THE RUBY PENDANT

Cleopatra's Legacy 2

Dorine White

ISBN: 1493775340
ISBN 13: 9781493775347
Library of Congress Control Number: 2013921237
CreateSpace Independent Publishing Platform
North Charleston, South Carolina

Praise for

The Ruby Pendant

"Rich with atmosphere, and full of delightful shivers, The Ruby Pendant pulled me right in. Part mystery, part ghost story, it is completely enjoyable."

- BRADEN BELL, author of the Middle School Magic series

"The Ruby Pendant is a non-stop thrill ride through the heart of New Orleans and beyond. A great read for adventurers of all ages."

- JENNIFER SHAW WOLF, author of Breaking Beautiful and Dead Girls Don't Lie

"Secret rooms! A missing necklace! Ghosts! The Ruby Pendant is a thrill-ride through New Orleans, a creative blend of suspense, mystery, and historical tidbits sure to tantalize readers of all ages. A worthy sequel."
- LAURISA REYES, Editor-in-Chief of Middle Shelf Magazine

For Mom and Dad, who always believe in me.

CONTENTS

1

FEELING BLUE?

M elanie twirled the turquoise bracelet around her wrist, watching the blue beads swing around like ponies on a carousel. She'd stolen it just that morning from her Aunt Florence's jewelry box. Aunt Flo wouldn't mind, she was dead, but Uncle William, that was a different story.

If he found Melanie rifling through her aunt's things, he would kill her and then hang her up in the front window as a warning to all meddlers. Well, not really. But she would probably be grounded for life. Aunt Flo's room was off-limits. No entry. An actual shrine.

Right then Melanie sat squished in the back seat between her mom and uncle as they rode to church. The ride was taking for-ev-er. Her uncle patted Melanie's knee reassuringly. Today he sported a dark-blue suit and vibrant, purple tie. Melanie had always thought of him as a young man, but since Aunt Flo's heart attack three years ago, he had started to look every minute of his fifty-eight years.

When they arrived at church, Melanie waited for her mother to get out of the car and then approached Saint Mary's colossal front steps. She watched as her mom's long, blond hair swung back and forth over her almost-bare back. People often told Melanie she took after her mom. With precise steps and a slight swagger, her mother called attention to herself with every movement. Yep, that was Ms. Rosanne Belaforte, though her mom refused to use her married name anymore and now went by Dufour, her maiden name.

Melanie still used her full name. Her fists clenched as she felt the pings of that particular pain rekindled. Divorce did not mean that her dad did not exist. She couldn't wait to spend time with him over the summer. He was a law professor at Penn State. She still thought of her parent's romance as dreamy. They'd met at college, her dad a promising young law student, and her mom, an interior design major. When they married, the world had been a jumble with possibilities. Some of the top law firms in the country had sought Melanie's dad. Melanie remembered living in New York when she was younger, going to Central Park and visiting the zoo.

It all fell apart when Melanie turned eight. Her dad decided he loved teaching the law, not practicing the law. If Melanie closed her eyes really tightly, she could still hear the screaming. Her mom wanted to live the life of a lawyer's wife, not a schoolteacher's. It had broken Melanie's heart when her parents divorced. Now she only got to see her father on some holidays and for part of the summer. She missed him so much.

The walk from the car to the church always felt like being part of a parade. As they took their places in line, the other performers arrived.

As they continued up the cathedral steps, Melanie shook her head at the pageantry of it all. Soon the old, oak doors rose in front of her like guardian angels. As she passed from sunlight into candle-lit darkness, the smell of musty incense floated in the air. Things brightened up considerably as they made their way toward the apse. Crystal chandeliers hung like dewdrops from the high rafters, and as the sun shone in through the stained-glass windows, the cathedral sparkled with rainbows of color.

Melanie followed her mother and Uncle William, who cut an elegant profile. Even though he was a little overweight, an air of dignity hung around him. They sat in the same pew every Sunday. It angled toward the front, allowing them to see the other parishioners as they approached the altar for Communion. Though the bench rested only twenty feet away, it took ages to be seated. Her mother had to stop and shake hands with someone in every row.

Melanie hummed as she waited; casually taking note of what everyone was wearing. She needed new pieces to add to her art portfolio. She would sketch them later, when she had the time.

When they finally took their seats, there were still plenty of open pews in the vast cathedral, so she was surprised when she felt the weight of a person sitting down beside her."Hello," Melanie said, turning, but there was no one there.

That's strange. She glanced behind her, but saw only an elderly couple engrossed in conversation.

Troubled, Melanie tugged on her mother's shoulder. "Mom?"

"Shhh!" hissed her mother, and then with a side-glance, she said, "Sit up straight."

Organ music filled the building, and soon the smell of fresh incense hung over the pews. Melanie brushed aside her worries as Father Patrick climbed the wooden steps to the pulpit, his black robes trailing on the floor. The choir fell silent.

Melanie loved this part. She closed her eyes and listened as the priest prayed in Latin. However, the feeling of peace only lasted until the service ended.

Outside, her mother took her elbow, leading her through the crowd of gossiping women. Melanie knew exactly where they were headed. Pierre Cerise and his two daughters had entered the service late. His wife had died several years ago, but he was finally back on the market, and Rosanne's intentions toward him were obvious. With his family name came both old money and new prestige. Handsome and connected, he was her next step up the social ladder.

"Pierre, darling." Rosanne's voice dripped like melted chocolate.

"Rosanne, what a pleasure," said Pierre, lifting her hand to his lips and kissing her wrist.

Yuck. Melanie tried to look away but Thing One and Thing Two captured her attention. Pierre's twin daughters, Charity and Grace, were staring daggers at her. Both girls were wafer-thin with delicate, white skin and long, dark hair. *What is their problem?* Melanie eyed them back. They were both like cold fish—highly fashionable marine life, to be sure, but still frigid and mean. Tomorrow she would be stuck with them again, finishing eighth grade at Her Lady of Grace Preparatory School. Luckily, it was a short week. They got off early on Thursday to prepare for Mardi Gras.

All three girls stood still while their parents talked. Thankfully, Melanie soon heard the deep baritone of her Uncle William's voice. Silently she urged him to hurry along—she really wanted to leave, but he didn't reach them soon enough. Melanie's mom was making plans for a joint family picnic in two weeks. *Oh, the horror.*

Finally, she felt her uncle's hand on her back. They were turning to go, and for one glorious moment, Melanie thought she had made it through the encounter unscathed, but Charity and Grace were skilled.

"What a beautiful tote bag, Melanie," Charity squealed.

Before Melanie could move away, Charity's fingers grasped the straps of her tote and pulled it off her shoulder.

"Oops, my fault," Charity said, simpering, all sugar and sweetness as the bag fell from her fingers.

Melanie felt the straps drag across her wrist, snagging on the turquoise bracelet. With a wrench, the bag pulled the bracelet off, and both fell to the ground.

I'm dead.

Melanie's feet froze while her brain yelled for her to pick up the bracelet. Her uncle moved faster. Before she knew it, he had everything in hand. In seconds, her stuff was back in the tote—all but the bracelet and sketch pad. Melanie's heart stopped.

"What a beautiful bracelet, Melanie. Where did you get it?" her uncle asked.

"Ah." Her mouth hung open.

"And this leather album. What splendid scrollwork. Are you using this for your sketching?"

"Um, yeah."

"Wonderful. Just wonderful." Her uncle slipped the sketchbook into the tote and slung the straps over her shoulder. "Melanie might only be thirteen, but she's quite talented," he said, holding the bracelet out to her.

"Of course she is," said her mother. "She's a Dufour."

"You mean a Belaforte," said Melanie. Her mother's disapproving look could have shattered glass, but Melanie didn't care.

As they walked toward their car, Melanie gripped the tote tightly. She had been lucky this time, but she needed to put the bracelet back ASAP.

2

SECRET PLACES

M elanie sat on her bed sketching and waiting until the house was quiet. She drew from memory the people from church. Characters came to life: Mrs. Badger with her deep-blue, two-piece suit; Jessica in her beautiful, spring dress; and little Tami May in a puffy dress covered with bold flowers.

Her bedroom was her sanctuary. Artwork crowded her walls, sketches and pastels from her own collection. Large movie posters, for films such as *Gone with the Wind* and *Casablanca*, covered the rest. When the clock blinked midnight, she placed her sketch pad on the nightstand and quietly opened her door.

Quiet as could be, Melanie tiptoed down the hallway and into Aunt Flo's room. In the dark, the room appeared eerie. Shadows covered everything. The only light came from the half-moon hanging outside the window. If she turned on the light, she would surely be caught. So instead, she picked up the jewelry box and sat with it on the floor.

It took a while to untangle all of the necklaces she'd left twisted together from her quick search that morning, but finally Melanie had everything in order. Even the turquoise bracelet was back where it belonged. She stood, balancing the jewelry box in her arms.

CREAK.

The old, wooden floorboards settled. Melanie slipped over to the dresser and placed the jewelry box right onto its empty dust outline. With a glance over her shoulder, she tried to even out her breathing so she could hear if anybody was coming. The house was quiet.

Melanie turned to sneak out, but her big toe snagged the edge of the rug, and she fell forward. She had a second to study a beautiful landscape painting spotlighted in the moonlight before she smashed head first into it. *Uff!* The frame tilted sideways, and her body hit the ground with a thud.

Stupid floor! What did I ever do to you? Melanie struggled to sit up, but the noise she caused made her freeze in place. If her uncle had heard it, he would be all over her in seconds. Her heart pounded against her rib cage as she listened for footsteps. Seconds passed, and then she let out a pent-up breath. No one was coming. As silently as possible, she untangled her arms and legs. She felt as if she was moving through peanut butter, but she was being careful this time. She critically eyed the painting. There was one small scratch. Just one. Nobody would notice it if she put everything back to normal. With slow movements, she shifted the frame back into place. *Whew.*

All was well until a whirring, grinding sound erupted from behind the painting. Gears shifted, and wood scraped against wood. *Did I trigger an alarm?* Melanie was already stepping away when the wall beside the painting suddenly slid back, revealing a three-foot gap. She jumped, and then...

The whirring sound stopped, and all was quiet again.

Melanie glanced between the safety of the bedroom door and the unknown of the empty space. She knew that she couldn't leave the secret door open, so with shaky steps, she inched toward the opening.

The closer she got to the dark entrance, the more she felt like she might vomit. She'd never been so scared in her whole life. Her hand trembled and shook as she placed it on the doorjamb. Slowly, she eased her head around the corner to peek into the void. When she saw no dead bodies or ghouls of any kind, she let out her breath and took a step forward. She was inside a secret room.

A beam of moonlight floated down from a high window, illuminating a small parlor. *Was this Aunt Flo's study? Why didn't she ever tell me about it? Maybe this is why Uncle William doesn't want me playing in here.*

Dust blanketed the room. The air felt thick and smelled of old papers. Melanie's nose hairs tickled as little dust fibers floated past her through the air. ACHOO!

I'm really pushing my luck now, she thought as she baby-stepped further into the study. In the semidarkness, she could make out floral wallpaper and a small settee. The room was only six feet wide and seven feet deep, but the ceiling rose high, giving the illusion of space. An oak bookcase stood against the other wall. Melanie glanced at the books cramming its shelves. She could smell the musty pages from where she stood. *Ick.*

The mystery of the hidden room tickled her curiosity, but her conscience was telling her to get out fast. Melanie hesitated, uncertain, biting her lip in frustration. She couldn't help herself. The secret room tempted her, spoke to her. Unable to resist, she skirted around the little coffee table and, in two steps, she was at the bookcase.

In the dim light, it was impossible to read any of the book titles. Melanie tried to pull one out to get a better look, but it was stuck to the next one. Her nerves exploded inside of her. She tried another book, and another, but Melanie's hands shook so badly she couldn't separate any of them. Frustrated and frightened, she turned to leave, but then she spotted something she hadn't noticed before, a book on the coffee table.

This single book was perfect for her to grab. She touched the cover. It felt old and dry, leathery. With careful fingers, she picked up the book and opened it. The binding crackled, protesting the intrusion. Melanie angled the pages into the moonlight, trying to read the writing. She couldn't quite make it out, but spidery script covered the pages like a lace doily.

The text was beautiful but hard to read. Melanie squinted and then gasped. She'd found her Aunt Flo's diary. *I should tell Uncle William. Wait! Stupid idea. Then he'll know I've been in here.*

With no time to waste, she hugged the book to her chest and scurried out of the hidden room. At the bedroom entry she stopped, remembering that the secret door remained wide open.

She raced back to the wall opening and scanned the sides, looking for levers or buttons, but there was nothing. Melanie gazed around in panic. She tried using her fingertips to pry the door shut, but it didn't budge.

Think, Mel. Think. She bounced her fist off her forehead, desperate for inspiration. Then she had it. *The painting*! She reached out and moved the frame. The whirring began again, and the door slid shut.

With the journal in hand, Melanie went back to her room, amazed that she hadn't been caught. *Note to self: I'd make a terrible thief.*

3

GHOSTS AND OTHER THINGS THAT FLOAT

Cool fingertips brushed across Melanie's forehead. Deep in sleep, she rolled over, unconsciously sensing another presence in the room. A chill worked its way down her arm, and she awoke, not knowing why.

Blinking heavy sleep from her eyes, Melanie peered around in the darkness. The tick-tock of her clock echoed throughout the bedroom. All else was silent. Pale moonlight struggled to enter the room from behind closed curtains. It was not enough light to see by, but it was enough to know she was alone.

With a sigh, she laid her head back on the pillow, hoping sleep would reclaim her. Just as her eyes fluttered closed, a cold kiss brushed her forehead.

Melanie screeched. She flung off her covers and sat up.

An eerie, white figure floated two feet in front of her bed. It rose and fell as if it were being tossed upon a breeze. A milky white arm stretched toward Melanie.

"Holy moly!" Melanie bounced off her bed. She backed away, holding her pillow out like a shield. She felt as if she might faint, and she desperately wanted to be anywhere but there.

Help...help! Melanie couldn't form any words. Her mouth had gone completely dry. If she didn't pull herself together, she'd start mumbling like a fool. The ghost continued to float up and down, but didn't come any closer. As Melanie backed toward her door, she searched for a weapon, trying to be brave.

"Stay back, I've got..." She glanced down at the floor. "I've got a slipper!" She snatched it up from the carpet. The foolishness of her threat flitted through her brain, but fear blocked everything else. The cool metal of the doorknob dug into her back, halting her retreat.

The apparition continued to hover. As Melanie reached behind her back to turn the doorknob, the ghost formed into the figure of a woman. Its hand lowered.

Melanie had lived in New Orleans since the divorce, surrounded by the superstitious. She had heard all the tales of voodoo, witches, and ghosts, but she had never believed them. In fact, she could remember many times when her mother would hasten her along the Boulevard, passing little stores with tarot cards or dead chickens in the windows. She had thought the people in those stores were bizarre and irrational, but she had never been scared of them, as her mother seemed to be. They were just a part of the flavor of Louisiana, like hunting gators or touring graveyards. Now her fear told her it was time to rethink things.

The doorknob behind her wouldn't turn. *What do I do?* She was stuck—in her room—with a ghost! Melanie shook her head and bit her lower lip. "What do you want?" Her voice trembled.

The floating body pointed at her once again. The hairs on the back of Melanie's neck rose like porcupine quills. "Me? You're here for me? Are you sure?" She tried the doorknob again. There had to be some way out of this.

The spirit shook its head. Melanie breathed a sigh of relief. "Then what do you need? Do you want me to do something?"

The presence bobbed its head. Wisps of white vapor escaped the form as it moved.

"OK. Can you talk? Can you tell me what you want?" Melanie began edging along the wall, heading for the bathroom door. Maybe she could escape that way. Peeking over her pillow, she waited for the ghost to respond. Instead, it moved.

Melanie took a quick side step and bumped into a lamp. The ghost glided past the bed, stopping near Melanie's headboard. It reached its fingers out and pointed.

A tingle spread down her spine as Melanie noticed that the spirit did not reflect in the wall mirror. *Wasn't it vampires that cast no reflection?* The ghost seemed to quiver. It gestured frantically at the bed.

"All right, already," said Melanie. However, the only way to get to her bed was to pass around the ghost. She held her breath as she eased by the spirit. The air felt cold, and goose bumps broke out on her skin. She moved one of her pillows. Beneath it rested the old, leather diary.

She turned to the ghost. "The diary? You want the diary?"

The spirit shook its head and pointed from the journal to Melanie.

"You want me to read the diary?"

The presence nodded.

Melanie held up the book. As soon as she touched it, she noticed a change in the atmosphere. Her bedroom felt warm and cozy once more. She looked around for the ghost, but it was gone. The relief she felt was enormous, as if a ten pound crushing weight had lifted. She switched on her lamp, and then, sitting on the bed, she slowly opened the diary.

Something must be done. I, Florence Dufour, write these words in my own hand. Beware!

Chills spread from the book to Melanie's fingers and coursed through her body as she read. *Creepy! Aunt Flo? What had she gotten herself into?*

Melanie had always loved Aunt Flo. As a child, she thought her aunty was silly and would laugh and giggle at her. She never understood why her mom and her uncle seemed so worried about that, but the woman had a real flare for the dramatic. She and Melanie were always up to some sort of mischief together. Aunt Flo would often let her play dress-up with her clothes and cosmetics or take Melanie on walks. They'd had so much fun together.

It was not until Melanie was much older that she noticed her aunt's strange mood swings. They would be having a tea party when suddenly her aunt would shush her into silence and tilt her head as if she was listening to something. She always seemed distracted, but things got much worse during the last three years of her life. That's when she started yelling at strangers in the park. Melanie would be so embarrassed. Most of the time, people would look as if they felt sorry for the crazy, old lady; but every once in a while, someone would pay attention to her. That was when things got weird. She'd be telling the person off, and he would just freeze in place, staring in horror. Then he would shake his head in denial and walk away, often pale and trembling. A few people just took off running, never looking back.

Once, after a bad episode, Melanie asked her aunt why she yelled at people. Aunt Flo glanced at her sadly and whispered, "They shouldn't think those kinds of things." Melanie never understood, and soon after, her aunt was confined to the house, and the outbursts decreased. In fact, most of the time, things were pretty normal. But how normal can life be when you know your aunt's gone crazy?

Melanie wasn't sure she was ready for this. Did she want to read any further? What would the world look like to a deranged mind?

She didn't take more than a moment to ponder that question before the urgency of the ghost resurfaced in her mind. With a shiver, she bent her head to the task. She would confront the madness.

Several hours later, and just as the sun brought the dawn, she reached the end. But what was the point? It didn't make any sense. Her aunt had obviously been loopy. Over and over, she had described different times when voices told her to do things, go places, or just call someone on the phone.

At one point, she wrote about their neighbor, Mr. Boulet. She'd filled pages describing what a sinful man he was and how one day he would get what he deserved. The weird thing was that Aunt Flo had never met him. Mr. Boulet had moved into the neighborhood after she had been confined to the house for psychiatric reasons. Why would she write pages and pages about that man?

Toward the end of the diary, things got even weirder. She had written odd things, such as "Beware the necklace" and "Something must be done." What was that supposed to mean? The only necklace that Melanie remembered her aunt wearing was the one Uncle William had given her for their twenty-fifth wedding anniversary. It was a beautiful ruby pendant. Uncle William had found it on a trip to England and held onto it for years, saving it for their silver anniversary. Aunt Flo loved it. She never took it off, but somehow she'd lost it. As Melanie thought about it now, she realized how strange it was for her aunt to misplace something so precious. *If she never took it off, how could it have gone missing?*

Melanie remembered reading something in the diary that struck her as odd. She flipped back until she found what Aunt Flo had written. *"Beware the necklace. I've finally done what needed to be done. Only death shall lend a hand."* Things were getting way too creepy. Had her aunt done something with the pendant?

Melanie closed the journal and snuggled into her pillow. Her nerves were shot, and she was exhausted. *Now what do I do?* She needed help, but whom could she let in on her secret?

Mom and Uncle William are out. They'd punish me for snooping. And I can't trust the girls at school with anything this big. There was really only one person she could ask—Sybil.

Sybil was the cook's daughter and had been Melanie's best friend until Mel had gone off to prep school. They'd done everything together. Melanie fondly remembered painting each other's toenails and sharing secrets about boys. Aunt Flo had even let them play dress-up together. Tragically, that is what ended it all.

Melanie's mom had caught them running around the garden in a couple of Aunt Flo's designer dresses. Melanie had never seen her mother's face turn so red. She was sent off to private school the next week, and only allowed to come home on the weekends. It was her mom's way of ensuring that Melanie would find "more appropriate" friends. At first, she and Sybil had still played on some weekends, but soon their worlds grew apart. Melanie was enrolled in cotillion classes while Sybil hung out at the community center. Evidently, Melanie was destined to be a debutante. She didn't care for it much, though the clothes were cool. But it was important to her mother, so she didn't have much of a choice. *Will Sybil want to help me after all this time?* Melanie wondered.

She knew that Uncle William planned to go golfing this Friday. She would call Sybil when she got home from school on Thursday. That decided, she closed her eyes and tried to sleep. Now her only concern was whether her old friend would pick up the phone.

4

BEST FRIENDS FOREVER?

Luckily, Sybil not only picked up the phone, but also agreed to come over. She arrived right when she said she would. Nervous, Melanie was peeking out the window. It had been a long time, but Sybil appeared to be well. Her coffee-brown, Creole skin and curly, black hair shone in the sun. Her family had lived in New Orleans for generations.

Melanie opened the door. "Thank you for coming," she said.

"I was curious," replied Sybil, frowning.

Melanie sighed. This would not be easy. Sybil still blamed her for ruining their friendship. Their final blowup had stemmed from the same old argument. Sybil knew that all the drastic changes were because of Melanie's mom, but she still blamed Melanie for going along with them. True friends would have stuck together, and Melanie had failed.

"This better be important," said Sybil.

"Important? You could say that. Let's go into the family room. You should probably sit down when I tell you."

With a glare, Sybil turned and headed to the entertainment room. Melanie was beginning to wonder if Sybil was only there to rub Melanie's nose in guilt. Sybil's mom was the cook for Melanie's family, so it was not as if their families were disconnected. But Melanie hoped that some of their old friendship was buried away somewhere. It had been over three years, but now Melanie knew that Sybil had been right. At the private school, Melanie had learned that true friends were hard to find. As she followed Sybil through the hallway and into the TV room, her mind was whirling with ways to apologize.

Melanie loved this room. Large, comfy sofas and chairs took up most of the space. Huge tapestries hung on the walls, and a plush carpet covered the floor. Dead center on one of the walls was a large, flat-screen TV. It was like her own private movie theater.

Sybil took a seat in one of the chairs while Melanie paced, moving her fingers in an awkward rhythm, not knowing where to start.

"Is it cold in here, or is it just me?" asked Sybil.

Behind Sybil, the air grew misty. Melanie watched wide-eyed as a shadowy form condensed two feet behind her old friend. It was the same ghost from before!

"What is it? What's wrong?" asked Sybil.

Melanie hadn't realized she'd been backing up. She froze, unsure how to answer. She wanted to run, but if she did, Sybil would be alone. She didn't want to make the ghost angry, and she didn't want it to do anything to her friend. So Melanie plastered a grin on her face, determined to play it off. If Sybil saw the ghost, she might run away and not come back. Melanie needed Sybil's help. "Nothing's wrong," said Melanie "Just... thinking."

Trying to keep the alarm off her face, she continued to watch as the spirit took shape. The ghost seemed more defined this time, and somewhat familiar too. The spirit rose up into the air, floating high above Sybil. It pointed down and then pointed at Melanie. Was the presence telling her that Sybil was a good choice? The apparition nodded and then simply vanished.

"Your air conditioner must have issues," said Sybil. "Now it's getting warmer."

"You have no idea," said Melanie.

"So, are you going to tell me why I'm here or do I have to guess?"

"If I share something with you, you have to promise you won't think I'm crazy."

Sybil laughed. "Don't worry. Nobody could be as crazy as your aunt."

Ouch!

"About my aunt, well, this was her journal." Melanie held up the diary. "I found it in a secret room." She glanced at Sybil, but there was no mocking in her old friend's eyes, so Melanie continued. "I know everyone thought Aunt Flo was a little different because she tended to carry on conversations without anybody else in the room."

Sybil snorted.

"I've been reading her diary. Most of the entries are nonsense, but every now and then I have the feeling that there's more here. I'm just missing it."

"What does that have to do with me?" asked Sybil.

"Well," said Melanie, "I need someone to help me figure out the journal."

"And my name just happened to come to mind?" Sybil's expression was tight.

"Look Sybil, I'm sorry for what happened before. You were right, and I was wrong. I know that doesn't fix anything, but when I tried to think who I could ask for help, you were the only one I thought of. I can trust you, right?"

Sybil did not speak for a moment. When she did, her stare was softer than before, but her voice was still chilly. "What kind of stuff did your aunt write about?"

Melanie showed her the diary and the warning about the pendant. "Isn't that creepy?"

"I wonder what she meant by 'only death shall lend a hand.'"

"I wondered that too," said Melanie. "It actually seems like a puzzle. At the very end, before she died, she wrote about following the clues. I haven't figured that part out yet. Oh yeah...and there's one more thing," Melanie paused. "I'm being haunted by a ghost."

"A ghost?"

"Yep," said Melanie.

"Well, that explains the temperature problem in here."

"You're not scared?"

"Nope. There are ghosts all over the place. We live in New Orleans, for goodness sake."

Melanie's grin widened. "Well, Mom is at a volunteer meeting, and Uncle William is playing golf. Now's the perfect time to look through Aunt Flo's old room—if you want."

"Fine. I'll come with you, but it doesn't mean everything's OK with us. Understand? You've just got me curious. That's all."

Melanie bobbed her head. She'd take whatever she could get.

They went up to the second floor.

"Aunt Flo and Uncle William had separate bedrooms for a while," explained Melanie. "Hers was down this way. It's where I found the diary."

"Sounds like a good place to start," said Sybil.

They looked around Aunt Flo's bedroom. Everything was where it should be. "We have to leave everything in its place or Uncle William will know I've been in here," said Melanie.

"No problem."

"Let me show you the secret room. Maybe there are some clues in there." Melanie walked over to the picture hanging on the wall. With a flip of her hand, she moved it to the side and then back into place. The hidden door swung open beside it.

"Wow." Sybil stared in amazement.

"I know, right?"

The room wasn't nearly as forbidding in the daylight. Melanie gestured for Sybil to follow her.

"Well, this is it. I found the diary on the coffee table. There's not much else in here but the bookcase."

"Then let's check out the books," said Sybil.

They each grabbed an armload of books. Some of them were stuck together, but they just bundled everything and continued their search. Book after book turned up nothing, and the dust made Melanie sneeze.

"How long will your mom and uncle be away?"

"Geez, I totally forgot." Melanie pulled out her cell and checked the time. "It's OK. We've probably got another thirty minutes, but I wouldn't press our luck any longer than that."

Sybil laid the book she had just flipped through onto the pile of rejects. The image on the cover triggered bells in Melanie's brain.

"Syb, what was that last book?"

"Just a book on your family crypt. Why?"

"The cover just gave me an idea. You see that picture? That angel statue stands right in front of our mausoleum."

"So?"

"The clue, remember? It said death would lend a hand. And look. The angel is holding out its hand."

"Oh wow," said Sybil.

"We need to go there."

"Where?"

"The crypt."

"Hmm, might be fun," added Sybil.

5

WHAT LIES WITHIN

They found Jason walking down the hallway right outside the room. He was young, compared to the other
drivers they'd had, and Melanie thought he was hot! He
wore his navy-blue suit like a second skin.

"Hey, Jason, do you think you can give us a lift?"

"Of course. Where would you like to go?"

"To the family crypt."

Jason's eyebrow lifted. "Are you sure that's a good idea?
You know the kind of people that hide with the dead—
muggers and the like. You'd be much safer taking a tour."

"I've been there a thousand times," Melanie groaned.

"Fine, but I have to pick up your uncle from golf first.
Then I'll take you."

"Agreed," said Melanie.

When Jason returned, and Uncle William had stretched out for a nap, Melanie showed Sybil to the garage. Jason grabbed the keys to the Caddy, and they were off.

While driving past the beautiful Garden District, Melanie's thoughts began to wander. *Am I doing the right thing?* The beautiful scenery slid by, and the heady scent of flowers wove its way magically through the open windows, relaxing Melanie's nerves.

Sybil cleared her throat. "So, do you know where the crypt is? These cemeteries aren't places to mess around."

"I've only been there a few times," whispered Melanie.

Sybil shifted in her seat and gave Mel a withering look, but whispered, "I thought you'd been there a thousand times."

"That was for Jason's benefit. He's only been with us about a year. He'd have no way of knowing I was lying. Truth is, the last time I came was for Aunt Flo's funeral."

"Will you be able to find the crypt?"

"Trust me. You can't miss it."

They sat in uneasy silence as time passed. Finally they arrived at Lafayette Cemetery. Melanie stood outside the car looking at the massive graveyard with row upon row of tombs. She could understand why locals called it the City of the Dead. It was like a miniature metropolis with its own streets and houses. Statues covered the landscape, their varnish cracked and peeling.

"Would you like me to wait here?" Jason asked.

"Sure thing. We'll be fast," said Melanie. She turned to Sybil and motioned with her head. "Let's go."

They crept through a maze of tombs and crypts. Every blind turn made Melanie's heart thump. The monumental tombs were excellent hiding places for thieves. They passed from well-maintained crypts—nice and white, large and small—to low, crumbling, brick tombs, their white finish flaking off and weeds growing in the cracks.

Melanie tried to remember exactly where her family crypt stood. Once she saw it, she would recognize it for sure, so she paid attention to her surroundings.

Looking ahead, she saw Sybil rooted in front of a long wall. It stretched along the entire west side of the cemetery. Three horizontal rows of arched squares ran down the wall.

"Did you know they call them oven boxes?" Sybil asked.

"What?" Melanie called as she ran to catch up.

"They call the tombs oven boxes."

"That's disgusting."

Sybil only shrugged. "I guess it doesn't matter. The people are already dead."

"Sybil, you're freaky."

"Thanks."

They continued down another avenue of crypts constructed of different materials and in different sizes and shapes. They ranged from squat cubes to large walk-ins. Some even had fenced courtyards, balconies, and landscaping. After skirting a large palm tree, Melanie and Sybil came face to face with a decidedly odd-looking tomb. Covered in graffiti, rows of XXXs decorated the plaster. Colorful Mardi Gras beads were strewn about the raised doorstep, and small potted plants sat off to the side. Completing the picture were strategically positioned candles, melted down to nubs.

"Interesting," said Melanie. "It almost looks like somebody held a party here."

"I wouldn't be too surprised," said Sybil. "New Orleans never sleeps."

A loud wail of police sirens started blaring behind them, and both of them jumped in alarm. They turned and smiled sheepishly at one another. It was hard to believe that life went on in the city right outside the cemetery fence.

Finally, Melanie stopped in front of a large building. It took up two normal plots and looked like a small house with an iron fence wrapped around the exterior. In the center of its little courtyard was a giant statue of an angel—the same statue from the book. It extended its right hand in greeting.

"This is it. The Dufour family crypt," said Melanie.

Sybil rubbed her hands together. "Let's start looking. This should be fun."

"You have an odd sense of fun."

"I'm Creole. It's in my blood."

The iron gate creaked as it opened. Rust flecks dusted Melanie's fingertips, but there were no weeds poking up between the marble paving squares.

"Uncle William must have someone take care of the plot." Melanie wasn't surprised to see fresh flowers on the tomb steps.

"It's definitely better looking than the others around here," said Sybil.

They studied the outside of the tomb, looking for writing or obvious signs of tampering, but there was nothing. Next they checked the angel. It stood proud and tall, but there wasn't anything special about it either—no hidey-holes, secret compartments, or cryptic poetry.

"Looks like we'll have to go inside," said Melanie.

They approached the entrance to the crypt. A brass plaque hung beside the door on which name after family name was listed. Aunt Flo's name was at the bottom of the list.

It seemed sacrilegious to disturb the dead, and Melanie already had enough trouble with ghosts, but this was where the clues had led them. They had to do it. The door was heavy; it took both of them to swing it open.

Suddenly, a flood of cockroaches ran out the door and over their feet. Melanie jumped and let out a deafening squeal. When her heart finally slowed down, the buzz of flies filled her ears.

"I've changed my mind. Let's not go in."

"What? Scared of a few bugs?" Sybil teased.

"Yes! Absolutely, positively yes!"

"What did you expect? Flowers?"

"I hadn't really thought about it."

"Well, you'd better decide now. It's your quest."

Ugh! Melanie squared her shoulders and stepped forward. Inside, it was dark and creepy. "We should have brought flashlights."

Behind her, Sybil stumbled down a couple of steps before ramming into a marble bench. "Ouch!"

"Hold on one sec. I brought matches." Melanie fumbled around in her pocket.

"You could've said so before I stepped inside."

"Sorry," said Melanie. The rotten stench of the room almost drove her to her knees. "Yuck, did you bring a hankie?"

"No," squeaked Sybil. Melanie noticed that Sybil was pinching her nose. "Let's make this fast."

As Melanie moved around the room, little crunching sounds echoed with each step. She focused on finding the sconces, and not the bugs. She lit the candles one by one. Soon, the room glowed in the eerily flickering light. A bead of sweat dripped off her nose.

"It is way too hot in here," said Sybil.

"Yeah," Melanie agreed, "and that's so not helping the creepiness."

Aside from the bugs and the candles, now Melanie was looking at a tall, stone table with a body-sized, black, vinyl sack sagging on top. She could hear bugs scuttling inside the bag. Melanie gagged. She didn't want to think of Aunt Flo's body in there.

"Melanie, I thought you said this was your family crypt?" Sybil asked as she peeked around.

"It is."

"Then where's all your family?" Sybil gestured to the lonely body bag.

"Hmm, I don't know. I was only inside here once when they brought Aunt Flo."

"Maybe they cremate them?"

"I don't think so. Someone would have mentioned it," said Melanie.

They tiptoed around the room, afraid to make any noise. Melanie knew it was stupid, but she couldn't help herself. They peered into the shadowy corners, investigated all the alcoves and cracks, and finally checked out the body bag itself. Melanie's gag reflex was nearing full vomiting potential. She had to turn away. "I don't think I can do this."

"Maybe we should leave," said Sybil. "I mean, this is a little grosser than I thought it would be."

"That's a great idea," mumbled Melanie. "I can't believe we came in the first place."

On their way to the exit, however, Melanie glanced above the doors and stopped short. A small sculpture was tucked in an alcove above the entry. *Hello.* "Do you see that? There's a statue."

Melanie climbed on top of a stone bench to get a better look.

"Notice anything unusual about it?" Sybil asked.

Melanie stretch onto her tiptoes, but the candlelight did not reach up quite that high. "It's the same statue as outside, only much smaller." Melanie paused to blink the dust out of her eyes. "It's hard to see, but its hand points toward the body bag."

Melanie stretched up to touch the statue. She wasn't sure it would work, but she had an idea. She carefully pressed her fingers into the statue's hand, and CLICK. A puff of dust erupted from the opposite end of the crypt and, with a horrible grinding sound, a four-foot section of wall slid aside to expose the absolute darkness beyond.

"Good job, Melanie," said Sybil.

"Thanks, I was just thinking about Aunt Flo's words, how death would lend a hand. It seemed the natural thing to do."

They each grabbed a taper candle and bent to check out the passage. The candlelight illuminated only a few feet in any direction. With a sinking feeling, Melanie knew they would have to crawl inside.

"Now I really wish I had remembered a flashlight," said Melanie.

They inched their way forward across the dusty floor. Melanie despaired that her shorts would never be clean again. Sybil was the first to bump into something.

"Hey, Mel. I think I found something."

"What?"

"The rest of your family."

Melanie panicked and dropped her candle. "Oh, snap." The fallen candle sputtered out, and then she heard the gravelly sound that had accompanied the opening of the crawl space. Immediately, she scrambled back through the dark to where the door had been. The opening had sealed itself shut! She pawed at the wall, but it was no use.

She reached back around, her hands frantically brushing over the smooth cement as she felt for her extinguished candle. "Sybil? Did you hear that? We're totally trapped!" Finally, she felt the long, waxy stem. With a firm grasp, she held it up.

About a foot in front of her, she could see Sybil's back. Her candle's glow formed an aura around her body. Sybil crouched in front of a pile of sacks. Some were black vinyl, but most were old burlap.

Her friend's scared laughter echoed in the small room. "Aha. I remember learning about this in school," whispered Sybil. "You know how they make you learn state history? I just remembered something. There's a crazy law that only one body can be in a crypt at a time. When a new body arrives, they move the old ones out. I guess we know where they put 'em now."

"Makes gory sense," said Melanie. She held up her flameless candle. "A little help here?"

"Yeah, sure." Sybil leaned over and lit Melanie's candle again. The glow from both flames illuminated a larger area. "There's gotta be a clue in here somewhere. Let's look."

"But the door. Didn't you hear?" Melanie stammered.

"Yeah, I heard. I'm just trying to keep it together." Sybil stared with wide eyes.

"I think we're in trouble," said Melanie.

Sybil turned. The flicker of the candle cast strange shadows on her skin. "There's got to be a way out."

"Well, as soon as I figure it out, I'll let you know." Melanie slapped the floor with her palm. A plume of dust floated off the ground.

"You don't have to get snarky."

"Sorry," said Melanie. "I can only imagine the crud I'm sitting in. What a horrible way to die, all hot and dirty and gross."

"We're not going to die. I'm sure there's another switch in here. We came here for clues, right, so let's find one."

"Fine, but I'm not searching the bodies," said Melanie.

"The room is pretty small. We can just move things around. I don't think your aunt would hide anything in a corpse."

Melanie started looking to her right. It was hard to walk between the burlap bags with only a slight flickering flame to light the way. She gritted her teeth as her foot came down on a bag, and a sick, crunching sound echoed around the room. Most of the sacks were piled on top of each other. Melanie used her shoe to push one aside. She heard a tearing sound, and she watched in dismay as a dull, dusty bone slid through the bag's open seam. A bony hand landed on her foot.

She shrieked.

"What did you find?" asked Sybil.

"How can you be so calm? It is so horrible in here!" Melanie wailed.

"The sooner we find the clue, the sooner we get out. Besides, there's nothing I can do about it, and these people are already dead."

"Sybil, have I told you how bizarre you are?"

"A few times. Thanks."

"Ugh. I'm not seeing anything. What about you?"

"Nothing but burlap."

They searched in silence for a few minutes. Melanie tried to suck it up, but her mind kept throwing images at her. In one especially dark corner, she saw a bag that had split open and seemed to be moving.

Melanie rubbed her eyes. The bag trembled. Her mouth fell open, and she reached a hand back toward Sybil. Her words wouldn't come out.

Then, the bones began to vibrate. Melanie looked around frantically, hoping to see mice, or cockroaches, or anything rational, but...

The bones shook harder, some lifting off the ground like Mexican jumping beans. Melanie began backing away as the bones inched closer to each other. Piece by piece, the bones connected. Melanie watched as small bones fitted themselves together to complete a hand. A moan left Melanie's throat.

"Did you say something?" asked Sybil.

Melanie couldn't answer. She was watching a knee bone connect to a leg bone. Now with complete arms and legs, the skeleton slowly lifted itself off the floor, pulling the rest of its corpse from the bag. It wobbled as it tried to stand. Then, a thin, wispy film gathered around the bones, as ghostly skin emerged. Melanie noticed a distorted patch of space above the ghoul's right elbow. It seemed like a black triangle, but it was indistinct and out of focus.

"S-S-S." Melanie couldn't get Sybil's name to form. Instead, she felt her own legs tremble.

"Hey, Melanie, look over here," said Sybil.

Melanie turned her head ever so slightly, still keeping an eye on the skeleton as it reached into the burlap sack to find its missing head. A small squeak escaped her lips.

"Come on, Mel," said Sybil. "Stop sitting there and move your butt." Sybil turned, and her candle illuminated a tiny placard on the far wall. "It's the only other thing I can see that might be something. Do you think you can you read it without having to step on the bodies?"

Melanie quickly glanced at the placard, and then back again. The skeleton was now complete. Its eye sockets were deep, black pools of nothing that pinned Melanie in place. One bony arm, the one with the strange black shape, rose into the air and then pointed straight at Melanie. She watched the finger bones curl in toward the palm bones until only the pointer was left out, aiming at a target directly between her eyes.

The world seemed to dim like a black hole around Melanie, and she felt as if her soul was being ripped from her body by gnarly claws. She placed her hand over her heart, trying to calm the marching band in her chest and allow some air into her lungs.

"Yo, Mel?"

Sybil's voice broke the skeleton's dark hold over Melanie. For one brief second, the ghoul remained standing. And then poof! It was gone. All that remained was the half-open sack of bones lying unmoving on the floor. Melanie's entire body shook. She had to force her head to turn and look in Sybil's direction. She reached one hand out toward her friend, in a pose oddly reminiscent of the skeleton's. Her voice stuck in her throat, so she gurgled instead.

"What did you say?"

Melanie doubled-checked to make sure the bag of bones was still a bag of bones, and then turned again while clearing her throat. She followed Sybil's light and discovered the placard.

"Look. A clue!"

"Mel, I just said that. What's up with you?"

"Um. Nothing. I just didn't hear you the first time."

"Goodness, you're only a few feet away. Forget it. Just get over here and see if you can read the sign."

It must be the heat, thought Melanie. She forced the idea into her brain, passed the doubt.

"I think I can. Will you hold my shirt while I lean forward? I don't want to step on the bones to get to it."

So Sybil stooped behind Melanie and spread her legs for balance. Melanie leaned as far forward as she dared while moving her candle closer.

"It looks like a poem. Oh, wow! It's signed by Aunt Flo."

"Bingo!" said Sybil. "Can you read it?"

"One sec. It's hard to make out." She leaned forward even more, the fabric of her shirt stretching in Sybil's fingers. The candlelight moved along the plaque as she read:

My spirit cannot soar without you.

My heartbeat slows and fades.

The Blues makes lite my saddened soul.

Where Frenchmen walk I find my way.

A ripping sound split the chamber. Sybil yelped, and Melanie fell forward, her shirt torn at the seam. She closed her eyes as the burlap sacks rushed up to receive her.

One second passed, then two, and then...Melanie started laughing. "I'm OK." She choked on the dust as she righted herself. She had landed spread eagle over a large, bulky bag. "It's OK. It's only full of tools." She looked down at herself and shimmied back over to Sybil. "Well, at least I think it is."

Sybil lowered her hands from her eyes. "Wow. Good catch. Any thoughts about the clue?"

"Not off the top of my head. I'll have to think about it. And no offense, but I don't want to do it now. So, any ideas on how to get out of here?"

"Not a one."

The girls sat slumped against the unmoving wall panel. They could only watch as their candles grew smaller and smaller.

"Jason will come and get us," said Melanie.

"Sure, if he's not too late," Sybil answered.

"What do you mean, too late?"

"There's only so much oxygen in this room. And besides, I feel like I'm a roasted goose. Turn me over and my timer's probably popped out."

"Let's look around some more. I'm not dying in a nasty, old crypt."

"Oh, so now you change your story," Sybil said.

Melanie slouched and shimmied over several bodies. They both scanned the walls and ceiling again. As Melanie squinted, the skin between her eyebrows creased. She'd almost given up hope when she chanced to bump into one of the bodies. It sagged forward and slid down the wall into a lump on the floor. Instinct made Melanie jump forward to catch the skeleton, but she fell short, instead grabbing a piece of metal jutting out from the wall.

"What's this?" asked Melanie.

"Oh my gosh! You found it! Let's get our butts out of here."

With a quick thrust, Melanie pushed the lever up. The wall panel slid noisily aside, and a warm blast of rotten, oven-box air entered the room. They were free.

6

ATTACKED!

Melanie and Sybil left the tomb, wiping the sweat from their foreheads and whispering about the clue.

"It must mean something," said Sybil. "It's the only thing we've found that's obviously a clue."

"I know," Melanie said. "It's not the best poem in the world, either. It's gotta be a clue."

"You knew your aunt best. Any ideas?"

"Well, the heartbeat fading must mean death. That makes sense, being in a crypt and all."

"Soaring could be flying, or maybe...something up high?" suggested Sybil.

They were so intent on the discussion that they forgot to stay alert. Suddenly, Melanie's feet flew off the ground, and strong hands gripped her under the armpits. Too shocked to react, she was carried back several feet before the urge to struggle overcame her fright. Then she began flailing like a mad cat.

Sybil struggled in another stranger's grip, kicking and twisting. Melanie saw her smash her foot into her attacker's kneecap and heard him gasp, but he didn't let go.

Melanie couldn't break free either, so she started to scream. She'd had a lot of practice lately, and her vocal cords responded. Her voice carried over the graveyard and echoed around the tombs. "Jason! Jason, help!" The attacker tried to cover her mouth, but she bit him hard. "HELP!"

"Where is it?" Melanie's attacker snarled. "Where is the necklace?"

Melanie was too alarmed to answer. Struggling harder, she scratched at the man's arms, feeling soft flesh give way to her nails. One swift pull and the man's shirt cuff tore. Surprised at her strength, Melanie looked down to glimpse a black tattoo. It appeared to be a pyramid with a scarab beetle staring back at her. The image nudged at her brain, but she couldn't waste time thinking about it. Instead, she pulled away and back-kicked the guy right between the legs. He crumpled to the ground, moaning. She grabbed a loose piece of molding from a tomb and slammed it straight down on his head. The moaning stopped.

Meanwhile, Sybil's assailant had dragged her back toward the Dufour family vault. Melanie cautiously followed her friend's muffled screams. After guessing what the attacker's next move would be, she sprinted ahead and jumped onto a large, neighboring tomb. As the attacker went by, Melanie took a running leap, crashing into Sybil and the kidnapper. She felt the man let go of her friend as they dropped to the ground. The three of them landed in a heap, the culprit's head hitting a marble tomb with a noisy smack.

"Sybil! Are you OK?" Melanie shook her friend.

Sybil sat up, rubbing her bruised arms. "I think so," she said, catching her breath. "What if there are more of them?"

"I don't know. We'd better get back."

"The faster the better!"

They hurried back to the waiting car. As they approached the car, Jason came into view. He was casually leaning against the hood, smoking a cigarette.

"Mel, I don't think Jason heard the screams."

"How could he not? I screamed loud enough to wake the dead."

"I don't know. Maybe he's deaf."

"Let's get out of here before those guys wake up."

Everything was happening so fast that Melanie didn't know what to think. She had only just found Aunt Flo's diary, and now she was seeing ghosts and following clues. She was only thirteen. How was she supposed to cope with all of this? The most she'd ever had to stress about was which boy she'd ask to the prep school dance, but now...

They were almost to the car when Jason spotted them. Melanie pulled up short, and with a violent heave, she bent over and threw up all over the ground. Jason came running to the rescue, while Sybil held Melanie's hair back. It was awful.

"Sorry, I guess the adrenaline finally went away."

"No problem. Just keep it over that way," Sybil cautioned.

Jason's face was ashen as he looked them over.

"What happened?"

The girls exchanged looks and then turned back to Jason. "We fell," they said in unison.

He shook his head. "You know what? I'm going to believe you, because if it was anything else, I'd lose my job for sure."

"Perfect," said Melanie, and she opened the car door and let herself inside. From the backseat, she yelled, "Let's keep this our secret."

Outside the car, Sybil nodded while giving Jason the squinted eye.

"Trust me. Not a word will leave my lips." He held the door open for Sybil, and then stubbed out his cigarette with his shoe. The drive home was quiet.

Sybil's mom was working, so Jason dropped her off along the way, and then he helped Melanie sneak into the house when they got home. Now that Melanie was on her own, a shower was the first thing on her agenda. Her outfit would never again see the light of day.

Melanie didn't see Jason for the rest of the day, but he had obviously not breathed a word about their trip because Uncle William seemed pleasant during dinner.

That night, Melanie's mind swam in endless circles over the clue they had found. *Where do Frenchmen walk?* Melanie thought of the question over and over. The only answer that popped into her mind was the French Quarter, but she was forbidden to go there without a chaperone, especially during Mardi Gras. It was so unfair! All her school friends went, but Melanie? Oh no, it was too risqué.

It took awhile, but eventually she drifted off to sleep. She found herself deeply settled in a memory. It was strange how she knew it was the past, but at the same time, she felt herself in the present. She could see herself—only she couldn't have been more than eight years old.

"Melanie," said Aunt Flo, "be careful in those heels. I don't want you to twist your ankle."

The bedroom glowed with sunlight. Melanie wasn't supposed to be alone with Aunt Flo, but Aunt Flo was much more entertaining than the staff was. Aunt Flo was helping her play dress-up. She had lined up all her pretty shoes on the bed. Melanie had picked the ones with three-inch heels. She could barely walk in them, but she felt like a princess. She wobbled over to the wardrobe and pulled down a feather boa.

"Look, Aunt Flo. I'm a movie star!" she announced.

Her aunt glanced her way, smiling. "You're beautiful, my sweet."

Melanie spied a tube of lipstick on the vanity. She knew it was off-limits, but sometimes Aunt Flo didn't really know what was going on. She decided to make her way over to the vanity. Melanie plotted as she strutted back and forth at the end of the bed.

"Look Auntie, I'm on the red carpet."

No answer. Melanie watched as her younger self turned around, wondering why her aunt wasn't laughing with her. She peeked over at Aunt Flo, who was standing in the corner of the bedroom, waving her hands in the air and whispering to herself.

It was the perfect time for a little criminal mischief. Eight-year-old Melanie made her way over to the vanity. The tube of ultra-red 2000 lipstick was in her hands when Aunt Flo's cry made her drop it on the floor.

"Would you leave me alone?" Aunt Flo screamed.

Melanie glanced from the fallen lipstick to her aunt.

"I'm sorry, I didn't—"

Her aunt cut her off. She was not even paying attention.

"I told you I won't do it, so leave me alone."

Melanie stared at Aunt Flo, who was carrying on a two-way conversation with herself.

"Look, I can't help you. Go find someone else."

Aunt Flo began pacing the floor, irritated. She walked right past Melanie.

"Really, you are so annoying. OK, if I do it will you leave me alone?"

"Fine." Her aunt walked over to the bed and sat beside the telephone. She picked up the receiver and held it to her ear. Then, speaking into the air, she asked, "What's the phone number?"

She pushed the buttons on the phone and waited while it rang. Melanie stared at her, afraid to move. This was the exact reason she was not supposed to be alone with her aunt.

Aunt Flo spoke. "Hi, you don't know me, but I need to tell you something." Her aunt listened.

"I know it's strange, but I have a message for you. Well, it'll just take a second. You can do with it what you will." She paused. "The message is, 'The will is in the Snoopy cookie jar.' No, I can't tell you whom it's from. I'm just the messenger. Yep, and you're welcome. Good-bye." Her aunt hung up the phone, and then breathed a sigh of relief. "Finally."

Then she turned her attention to Melanie. "Don't even think about it, missy. That lipstick is not for you."

Eight-year-old Melanie laughed and went about her business, but older Melanie knew her dream was telling her something important.

7

UNWELCOME VISITORS

Melanie awoke suddenly, her heart racing. She just knew the ghost was in the room. In fact, it was tugging at Melanie's pj's. It couldn't truly grasp the fabric, but every time it tried, a cold pain shot up Melanie's arm. The ghost tugged and tugged. Melanie got the hint and jumped out of bed. She stared around the room, confused. What was the ghost up to? If only it could talk.

The ghost tried pushing at Melanie from behind. Melanie felt the cold touch all the way up her spine. The ghost was obviously in a hurry to get Melanie to go somewhere. She felt the ghost blow past her, and then stop at the bathroom door. Melanie didn't know what else to do, so she followed. Inside the bathroom, the ghost hovered at the adjoining door. Melanie took the hint and went through it, into the spare bedroom.

The room was dark and cold. The staff closed the vents in rooms not in use to save energy. Melanie looked around. There was nothing in the room besides old furniture. The house was dead silent. She could hear herself breathing. She glared at the ghost questioningly, but it seemed to be guarding the door back into Melanie's bathroom. Melanie started toward it, but the ghost expanded, rising off the ground in a threatening manner. Melanie took a step back. The ghost had seemed friendly until now. What had happened?

Creak!

Melanie heard the floorboards groan from her bathroom. Who was in there? She slowly advanced, and the ghost let her. Kneeling in front of the door, she placed her ear against the hard wood. She could hear movement on the other side. Whispering began. Melanie struggled to make out what was being said, but she only caught a few words.

"Girl...not...be," said one voice.

Another whispered back. "Good...we...find...it."

Melanie huddled on the other side of the door, listening as strangers searched through her room and bath. Why hadn't the security system worked? Where were the police? A terrible fear bubbled up inside her. Home was supposed to be safe. Home was where people loved and watched over her. She shivered in the cold air. Her life was turning upside down.

A crash from her bedroom drew her attention. They were breaking her things! She clenched her fist, wanting to yell and scream, but she was afraid she would be found. What if they'd already gotten to her mom and uncle? She glanced up at the ghost. Somehow, it had known danger was near and had saved her. The noises in her room slowly grew dimmer and then stopped. She hoped the thieves had left, but she was not going to check. They could be anywhere in the house. Her best bet was to stay put. She tiptoed to the old bed, crawled under the dusty comforter, and then curled up into a ball. She stayed that way until sunlight peeked through the curtains.

As she made her way back into her bedroom, Melanie could not stop the panic she felt. What had they done to her room? The bathroom seemed normal, besides all the drawers being open. She drew her breath before heading into her room. Behind the door, it was a mess. It appeared as if a hurricane had passed. Clothes were scattered across the floor. Bed linen hung off a chair, and the mattress lay on its side. Someone had taken a knife to the pillows. Fluff covered everything. Even her dresser drawers hung open. Tears ran down Melanie's cheeks.

Just then, the door swung open, and her mother walked into the room. She was checking her makeup in a compact and at first failed to notice the disaster. It was not until Rosanne stepped on pieces of a broken lamp that she paused and looked around in confusion. Her eyes grew wide.

"Melanie, what's going on in here?"

Relief surged through Melanie's chest. Her mom was safe and sound. She ran and flung her arms around her mom's waist.

"Mom, it was awful. Someone broke in last night. I was so scared. I hid in the spare bedroom." The tears flowed steadily.

"Oh my, Melanie! Why didn't you get help?"

"I was too scared. I thought they might have gotten you and Uncle too."

"My poor girl. Let's go call the police. This is unacceptable. Why do we pay all that money for a security system if they don't come when you need them?"

The police arrived quickly. They searched Melanie's room for fingerprints and clues, but they found nothing. Whoever had tossed her room had been thorough. The police asked Melanie all sorts of questions for which she did not have answers. Then they called the security company. Evidently, someone had shut off the alarm system manually around 2:00 a.m. The police interviewed all the servants. Her uncle was furious. He walked around the house with his chest puffed out and his face purple.

After the police left, the servants fixed up Melanie's room. She waited in the living room, dying to get back into her bedroom. Her mother kept herself busy by calling security agencies. They would soon have a house guard to back up the alarm system. Melanie was glad. Having another set of eyes around would make her feel much safer.

When Melanie finally made it back into her room, she peered around in wonder. The servants had done a remarkable job. If she hadn't seen the mess herself, she would have had no clue that anything had been wrong. Everything was back where it should be. All the broken glass was cleaned up, and new lamps and decor dotted the room. All her clothes were washed, folded, and returned to her drawers.

She wandered around, running her hands over the new bed linen and touching the new lamps. *Why did the thieves only target me? Oh no!* She ran to her dresser, throwing open the top drawer, and then pushed all of her underwear and socks aside. *No diary! It's gone.* She sat down on her bed, her shoulders sagging.

8

Voodoo R Us

Saturday afternoon, Sybil sat in the living room while Melanie told her tale.

"I bet it was the same guys from the cemetery."

"I think so too," said Melanie.

"They must have attacked in the graveyard thinking we'd found the necklace," said Sybil. "When they didn't succeed, they broke in here, searched your room, and found the diary."

"Yeah, but why now? And what's so important about the necklace, anyhow? Do they just want to pawn it?"

"Well, at least we know they don't have the necklace, but now they have the first clue."

"They'll head straight back to the crypt," groaned Melanie.

"We need to figure out the next clue so we can stay a step ahead."

Squeak.

"What was that?" asked Sybil.

"Don't worry about it. This place is so old that the whole house moans sometimes."

"At least the ghost showed up to protect you," said Sybil.

"Yeah, but what's up with the ghost? I can't figure it out."

"I think it's time we paid my aunt a visit," said Sybil.

"Your aunt? Why?" asked Melanie.

"Well, while the rest of my family went to church every Sunday, Aunt Cecile decided it wasn't for her and took up voodoo."

"You're kidding. I've never met anyone who practices voodoo. My mom walks to the other side of the street if she suspects anyone."

"Well, now's your chance. If anyone knows about spirits, it's a voodoo priestess."

"Jeez, I'm not sure. I really don't believe in all that stuff. And if my mom finds out, she'll kill me."

"It's not that bad. Come on. I sneak out to visit my aunt all the time. It's no big deal."

"OK, but no zombies or raising the dead," said Melanie.

"That's only in the movies."

"Yeah, right." Melanie's thoughts drifted back to the episode in the crypt. "You say that now, but when a zombie snacks on your brain, I'll be the first to say I told you so." She gave Sybil a cocky smirk and bumped her shoulder, but deep inside Melanie felt her stomach turn squishy.

"Whatever. Let's go."

Sybil took Melanie to a part of town that Melanie's mother would never approve of, if she knew. As Melanie glanced at the peeling, gray paint flaking from the wall of an apartment building, she almost stepped on a homeless man lying in the street. The comforting sounds of jazz music faded into the distance, and Melanie shivered. She had never guessed what a sheltered life she lived. Sure, New Orleans was famous for all its wonders, but Melanie never realized how much of the culture she had skipped.

They approached a two-story, redbrick building.

"Here we are," said Sybil. "Voodoo priestess central."

Melanie gave her a wary look before straightening her shoulders and stepping through the doorway. A hodge-podge of clutter greeted her. Everywhere she looked, shelves were crammed with candles, simply sewn dolls, skulls, crosses, and most alarming, snakes.

Fortunately, the pleasant smell of fresh herbs in the air released some of Melanie's tension. The tinkle of bells sounded to the left, and Melanie glanced over to find wind chimes hanging from a large armoire that was filled with jars of different sizes. She walked over to investigate, reading the faded labels that declared their contents: hummingbird hearts, lavender, frog legs—

"Can I help you?" a pleasant voice asked.

Melanie turned to see a small curtain part, and a tall, thin, black woman emerge. She appeared regal in a long, white dress and head wrap. It wasn't her beauty that struck Melanie though, it was the nine-foot-long boa constrictor wrapped around her shoulders.

Hiss!

Melanie took a step back.

"Aunt Cecile, this is my friend, Melanie. You remember her, don't you?" said Sybil.

"Of course I do, but back then she was barely as tall as my hip." Cecile beamed. "To what do I owe this nice surprise?"

Melanie stared passed the snake and into Cecile's eyes. "We need your help."

"Help?" Cecile asked. "I'm sure interested to know what kind of help you think I could provide."

"She's having a little problem with ghosts," said Sybil.

"Spirits. I see." Cecile's eyes narrowed at Melanie. "Does your mother know you're here?"

Melanie was pretty sure the voodoo priestess would know if she lied. "No, ma'am."

"Well, this must be a very interesting problem. Why don't you tell me about it?"

Sybil leaned back against the wall while Melanie did all the talking.

"Well," began Melanie. "It seems a ghost has attached itself to me. I don't really know why, but I think it has something to do with my Aunt Flo."

"Has the spirit done you or your loved ones any harm?" asked Cecile.

"No. In fact, I'm the only one who has seen it."

"Does it seem to want something from you?"

"I think it wants me to find my aunt's old necklace."

"Very interesting. Most spirits leave their physical cares behind. Hmm. What would you like me to do about this spirit? In voodoo, we believe that this world is extremely close to the spirit world, and that spirits often come to our aid."

"I don't know what to do. I was hoping for some advice. The ghost seems determined to have me find this necklace. The only problem is that someone else is after it, too."

Cecile glanced from Sybil to Melanie. The boa around her shoulders rose, its tongue flicked in and out of its mouth, and a deep rumble emanated from somewhere in its long body. The priestess began to pace the cement floor of the shop. The snake's agitation grew the longer Cecile paced.

"I do not have a good feeling about this. Spirits often come to protect us. This one seems to be worried." Cecile stopped in front of the armoire. She picked up a small, red, velvet bag and waved it in the air. "I'm going to make you a gris-gris bag. I think you might need more help than I can give. We will ask the spirits to aid us."

The priestess's slim fingers lifted jar after jar, sometimes placing a pinch of something into the velvet bag and other times returning the jar back to the shelf unused. She mumbled to herself as she went. "Python skin, yes, a little of that to unmask the truth. And perhaps two copper pennies for good fortune. Maybe lavender to protect her dreams, and hmm, let's see, a piece of iron for protection."

Clutching the bag tightly between her hands, Cecile closed her eyes and whispered a few quiet words. When she was done, she focused on Melanie.

"First, we need to cleanse you." The voodoo priestess pulled out a large cigar from behind a melted wax candle. As she lit it, the smell of tobacco filled the room, overpowering the basil. Melanie heard Cecile take in several deep breaths. Then moist, warm air floated around her. The smoke from the cigar floated over her body, weaving its way into her hair and clothing. When the puffing stopped, Melanie turned to face Cecile.

Sybil's aunt placed the gris-gris bag into Melanie's hands, and then covered them with her own. She then began swaying back and forth while speaking a small blessing of thanks to the spirits.

"There, that should do it. You either need to wear the bag or place it under your pillow."

"Um, OK." Melanie peeked questioningly at Sybil, and then back to Cecile. "Isn't there just a way you could make the spirit go away?"

The voodoo priestess shook her head. "That spirit is coming to you for a reason, and you need to discover what that reason is."

"Oh well. I guess it couldn't have been that easy."

"It rarely is."

Sybil finally stepped forward. "Thanks, Aunt Cecile."

Melanie turned toward the front door, dragging her feet. She had secretly hoped to vanquish the ghost and all her problems with it. Drat. She honestly didn't want to find the ruby pendant if it was going to be so much trouble. She twisted and came face to face with the portrait of a large, black woman wearing a red shawl and a bright-yellow turban. Dark, beady eyes seemed to look right through her.

"Ah, I see you've met Marie," said Cecile.

"Marie?" mumbled Melanie.

Sybil laughed. "For someone who lives in New Orleans, you sure don't know a lot about it."

"I've come to that conclusion all on my own, thank you very much," said Melanie.

"Melanie, let me tell you a little about Marie, the voodoo queen of New Orleans."

"Voodoo has a queen?" asked Melanie.

"That's just what we call her," said Cecile. "Marie was born way back in 1801. A free woman. Her first husband died kind of mysteriously, and after that, she gained notoriety as a spiritualist. The snake in the portrait is Zombi. She used it to perform ceremonies at night. People say she could divine the future and cure the sick."

"What happened to her?" asked Melanie.

"That's a good question. It was reported in the newspapers that she died in 1881, but many people claimed to have seen Marie after her supposed death. No one knows for sure. Many still visit her grave in Saint Louis Cemetery Number One and draw three Xs on the tomb to request wishes."

"That's what those Xs were! They were all over the place when we went to the family crypt," said Melanie. "I can't believe it."

"There are many who believe that spirits aid the living. I suggest you take your spirit seriously and follow its lead."

"Maybe you're right. Maybe it's about time to stop worrying over what I can't change and just do something about what I can. That ruby pendant must mean something significant," said Melanie.

"You two better hurry home before your moms start to worry," said Cecile.

Melanie left the store with a lot on her mind. She followed Sybil, rubbing her fingers over the velvet bag and pondering Cecile's words.

"I'm not sure about this gris-gris bag. It seems a little weird to me."

"So? It can't hurt," said Sybil.

"I don't know."

"It can only help."

"Fine, but I'm not wearing it. It'll clash with everything in my wardrobe."

"Ugh. You're hopeless," said Sybil.

"Please. You're the weird one. I'm on the up side of normal."

The streets became more congested as they neared the French Quarter, and Melanie had to dodge the tourists as they rushed here and there. Street musicians sat on the corners playing soulful music, their yearning chords echoing through the lanes. Melanie pulled Sybil to a stop at an outdoor café, selecting one of the small, round tables covered in crisp, white tablecloths.

"Let's sit and talk. I've got way too much stuff swimming around in my brain."

"Sure, I could use a Coke," said Sybil.

A mellow mood washed over them both as they sipped their sodas.

"Well," started Melanie, "I was thinking about the last clue. I wonder if it might have something to do with the French heritage in the area. I mean, it was the French and Spanish that settled the area."

"That's true. I was thinking maybe it had something to do with the French Quarter," said Sybil.

"The French Quarter is huge. How are we going to find a clue around here?"

"I can't come up with all the answers."

"I think we're going to have to visit all the jazz joints," said Melanie.

"Why jazz?"

"It was part of the clue. You know, the part about the blues filling her soul. She probably meant jazz."

"There are an awful lot of jazz joints down here. How do we know which ones to search?" asked Sybil.

"Actually, I was thinking of getting Uncle William involved."

"Why?"

"Well, every now and then, he gets all dreamy and emotional about Aunt Flo. He can go on and on about her, you know? If I ask the right questions, I'm hoping he can tell me if there was a box for that necklace. I bet I can get him to tell me about their favorite jazz clubs."

"That's definitely a good place to start," said Sybil. "How are you going to do it?"

"I'll try to get him talking over dinner tonight."

"Good luck."

"Thanks," said Melanie, "but hopefully, I won't need it."

9

EXTREME MEASURES

The dinner table sparkled with china and crystal. Dinner was a big deal in the Dufour household. Melanie sneaked in after Ms. Drew, the kitchen helper, had set the room and placed a bottle of one of Uncle William's favorite wines on the table. He liked them rich and red.

After stepping into the hallway, Melanie called everyone downstairs to dinner. She wanted the show to begin. Her mother arrived first, waving her hands over her hair, making sure every strand was in place. Melanie could never figure out what was so urgent about dressing for dinner. It was not like anyone special was there to see her.

Next, Melanie's uncle swaggered in. He paused, leaned against the doorjamb, and stared at the beautiful table. With a sigh, he went over to the head of the table, stumbling on the way.

"Ah, just what I need." He popped open the red wine and filled a tall goblet. When he raised the glass shakily to his lips, some wine sloshed over the side, leaving a blood-red stain on the white tablecloth. He swallowed half the glass in one gulp.

"Why William, whatever is the matter?" asked Melanie's mom.

"Darn vandals. That's what's wrong." He swallowed the other half of his wine.

Melanie began to doubt the idea of loosening Uncle William up tonight. He appeared pretty loose already. "What happened?" she asked.

"It's the family crypt." William slammed his goblet down on the table. "Some hoodlums broke into the vault. They upset my poor Flo. It's all thrown about. Who would do such a dastardly thing?"

Melanie opened and shut her mouth twice. She had a good idea who had done it, but she dared not bring it up. Just then, the maid carried a steaming tray of soup into the room. From the smell, Melanie guessed it was spiced squash—a favorite. Her uncle picked up a soup spoon but let it dangle from his fingers.

"My poor Flo." He dropped the spoon into the soup with a small splash. "When the police find these criminals, I'm going to make sure they pay."

Melanie took small sips of her soup. It was better for Uncle William to rant than to close down. She felt horrible. It was all her fault.

"Oh dear, oh dear," said Mom. "This is a bad time to share my news."

Uncle William ignored Mom's statement. Melanie would have, too. It was horrible timing, and just like her mom to put herself in the spotlight.

"I'm so sorry, Uncle William. Maybe it would help if you talked about the good times," said Melanie.

Uncle William leaned back in his chair, staring at the ceiling. The room was quiet except for the sound of her mother sipping soup.

"Florence was the most amazing woman in the entire world," said Uncle William.

"She was awesome," said Melanie.

Uncle William sat up straighter. He looked Melanie directly in the eyes. "Yes, she was."

"Tell me about her, Uncle William. I was so little."

"She was the life of the party," William began. "I don't know how I got so lucky. She chose me. Out of all the eligible men in town, she chose me. Everywhere she went, people laughed and enjoyed life. She sparkled."

"She liked jazz, didn't she?" Melanie asked.

Her uncle smiled, caught in the memory. "Oh, she loved jazz. She used to drag me down to the French Quarter all the time to hear this person or that new group. She sat in the cafés listening to the music, her eyes closed, and her body swaying. I used to sit and watch her. She loved it so much."

"Was there any particular place she liked better than the others?"

"Oh, it's hard to say. She loved them all. I'm sure I could remember if I stood in front of the shops, but I haven't been down there since she died." A veil of sadness fell over his face.

"Uncle William, do you think you could take me? Show me what Aunt Flo liked?"

That caught her mom's attention. "Certainly not! There is no way you are going down to the French Quarter during Mardi Gras season. There are all sorts of awful people down there."

However, the idea was planted. "Now Rosanne, I think that's a brilliant idea. I'd love to show Melanie around."

"But William—"

"No buts, Rosanne. Melanie's idea is fantastic, and she'll be with me the whole time. I'd love to show her some of my old haunts."

Melanie's mother slowly lowered her soup spoon to the table. Then she took the time to dab the corners of her lips with a napkin before placing it back on her lap. "If that's what you want, who am I to argue?"

Melanie knew her mother was playing a game, but Uncle William did not notice. "Great, it's all settled then. We'll go down on Monday."

Her mom's eyes narrowed. "Well, I guess I'd better tell you my news then."

Melanie braced herself. Her mom could let some doozies fly.

"The annual Ladies of the Revolution cruise is scheduled for the week after Easter. I know it's short notice, but we got a fantastic deal."

That's not horrible news, thought Melanie. *There must be more.*

"Pierre and I have been talking. We think it would be the perfect chance for Melanie to get to know Grace and Charity." Her mom smiled as she nailed Melanie with her stare. "We've decided you should stay with them for the week that I'm away."

"What? No way! You can't do that to me," said Melanie. She pushed back her chair and jumped up. "There is no way I'm going. I can stay here with Uncle William, just like always."

"No theatrics, dear. Everything is all arranged. Now sit down."

Melanie turned toward her uncle for help, but he was off in la-la land. She was stuck. "Mom, you're killing me."

"What happened to the sweet little girl who used to do what I said? I'm sure you'll have a fabulous time. Besides, a cruise means shopping, and I need you to help me pick out my wardrobe."

Melanie sighed. What had happened to the little girl who thought everything mom said was gold? "There's nothing I can do to change your mind, is there?"

"Absolutely nothing, dear."

"Well, in that case, I want at least a week's worth of new outfits out of this deal."

"Delightful. I knew you'd come around."

Ms. Drew entered the room to collect the soup dishes. Melanie's mother had the only empty bowl.

10

ALL THAT JAZZ

On Monday, Melanie woke up bright and early to pick out clothes for her day out with Uncle William. She was so excited! Finally, she was going to Mardi Gras, or Fat Tuesday as some people called it—the day when Catholics splurged before giving up something important for Lent. Actually, Mardi Gras was tomorrow, but the concerts, carnivals, and celebrations had already been going on for over a week. So Mardi Gras or not, it was party time!

Melanie had just put on the perfect outfit when her uncle tapped on her door.

"You ready, Melanie?"

"Am I ever!"

Jason drove them down to the French Quarter. Melanie had been on the outskirts of it all with Sybil the other day, but today would be different. Today she'd be a part of the action.

Her uncle gazed around with wide eyes. Melanie wondered what he was remembering. They walked side by side down Bourbon Street. It was like entering a magical kingdom. She could hear music coming from every nook and cranny. They stopped often, the narrow streets leaving little room for crowds of people to wander. Gray pigeons took up the rest of the space, pecking at the leftover crumbs littering the roads.

Melanie turned in one spot, capturing the chaotic scene. Voices, music, and laughter filled her ears. The rich smell of coffee flooded her nose. Ahead, two- and three-story buildings lined the streets. Wrought-iron railings wrapped around the different levels like protective fences, and people hung over the balconies waving at the crowds below. Bright and wild banners fluttered from iron posts, and flowering plants dotted every entrance. Melanie could feel the excitement thick in the air.

As they walked by a crowded street corner, Melanie pulled her uncle to a stop, trying to get a good look at all the commotion. Peeking around other people, she spotted an old black man, his chest covered with a dingy, metal washboard. A raspy sound scratched out as he played it with his fingertips. Next to him stood a large man pulling open an accordion. They had the entire crowd tapping their feet and clapping. The melody was contagious, and Melanie began clapping along, her head bobbing to the beat. Her uncle's eyes sparkled as he watched her, smiling his approval.

The energy running through the French Quarter was electric. Melanie followed her uncle, taking in all the sights and sounds. Her brain was on overload. They stopped at the Jazz Bistro. It had been one of Aunt Flo's favorites. While the waiter served them iced tea, Melanie peeked around for clues, but saw nothing.

She sat back and enjoyed the musicians playing in the front corner of the room. The sound of the trumpet bounced off the lively rhythm of the banjo, and every now and then, the cello would join in. All three musicians wore striped suits and white hats. Melanie couldn't imagine having a better time.

When they left, her uncle took her down another street. This one was much wider. In fact, over the middle of the road hung streetcar cables. People flowed back and forth between the shops and the sidewalk vendors, their arms full of packages. Melanie even spied artists painting people's portraits. She pulled on her uncle's sleeve, but he just laughed and continued forward. Everywhere she looked, people were busy.

Colors thrilled Melanie's senses. She had never seen blues so bold or reds so rich. Strings of lights and garlands crisscrossed above her, connecting balconies on opposite sides of the road. Their next stop was the Café du Monde. Uncle William showed her around, pointing out Aunt Flo's favorite table. Melanie kept her eyes open, but nothing seemed like a clue.

They walked farther, stopping at stages set up in alleys. Large awnings covered the platforms on which volunteer bands showed their stuff. On one raised stage, covered entirely in red, two grand pianos took up the entire space. Melanie wished she had caught the show.

On another stage waited a large, black woman, dressed to the nines. A row of men in black suits and sleek hats stood behind her. As the soulful sounds of jazz filled the air, the woman began to sing. Melanie held her uncle's hand, completely enthralled. The woman's voice was like chocolate silk.

It was plain to Melanie that Uncle William missed this part of his life with Aunt Flo more than she had guessed. She was so glad he could share it with her.

She was having the time of her life, but try as she might, she couldn't shake the feeling that something wasn't quite right. Melanie kept looking for clues, but the more she searched, the more she doubted there was anything to find. *What am I looking for?* It took her a long time to realize why she felt so uneasy.

Someone was following her. She could feel it. It had been nagging at her since they'd left the house. Sometimes the back of her neck would tingle, and she would turn, but no one was there. The feeling grew stronger as the day progressed, and she was beginning to get jumpy.

Distracted, Melanie bumped right into Uncle William when he stopped to watch a parade go by on a blocked-off street. New Orleans was famous for its scandalous Mardi Gras parades, but that was at night. During the daytime, high school bands marched. Kids carried banners, cheerleaders jumped around, and bands played songs. Melanie watched a large group of people coming her way. The women all carried fancy parasols, while the men carried black or metal umbrellas. Everyone danced while they walked, swinging their hips and stomping their feet to trumpet music. Melanie tapped her feet to the beat, humming along with the trumpet blasts.

Next came a single-story float covered in bright carnations. A man all decked out in vibrant purple stood on top, tossing beads to the people in the streets. Melanie caught a green necklace as it came sailing her way. As she slipped the necklace over her head, a shadow passed by her, and a chill tickled the back of her neck.

"Uncle William? Let's get going. I'm getting hungry."

"Sure thing. I know the perfect place. I used to take Florence there on our anniversary. It's a bit past the French Quarter, but not too far."

"Sounds good to me."

Melanie practically dragged her uncle down the street. As they got farther from the center of the French Quarter, the crowds diminished and Melanie's sense of comfort returned. They turned onto a street lined with novelty shops and cafes. The feeling here was less intense, calmer, and so Melanie slowed down and breathed in the atmosphere. A horse-drawn carriage clopped down the street in front of them. It was like no carriage Melanie had ever seen. It looked like a bus with four rows of seats, pulled by a massive horse.

As they waited for the carriage to pass by, Melanie casually glanced at the street sign. Her hand flew up to cover her mouth.

"Uncle William! This is Frenchmen's Street."

"So it is. Why?"

"Well..." She didn't know what to say, but in her mind she was connecting some dots.

Her uncle laughed at her serious expression, and then wrapped his arm around her shoulders and pulled her close. Melanie leaned into his side, the smell of his spicy aftershave bringing a grin to her face.

William led Melanie to a restaurant called Zydeco. *Wow.* Her uncle ordered some gumbo while she looked around at the interior of the restaurant. From the tables to the benches, everything was polished, yellow wood. Hundreds of old photographs hung on the walls. The patrons engaged in lively conversations while fast jazz music played in the background.

"Why did Aunt Flo like it here so much?"

"Ah, that's quite a story. You see, this is where she met Louis 'Satchmo' Armstrong, the king of jazz."

"Wow. I remember Aunt Flo playing old jazz recordings of his and dancing around her bedroom. This is amazing."

"Sure is. He even played her a song. No one could resist my Flo. In fact, there's a photograph on the wall somewhere of the two of them together. Florence donated it to the restaurant a few years before she passed."

Melanie's detective senses went on full alert. "Could you show it to me when we're done eating?"

"If I can remember where it is. They've added quite a few since I was here last."

Melanie wolfed down her food, but her uncle ate slowly, savoring every bite.

"So, you said you brought Aunt Flo here for your anniversary?" Melanie asked.

"Yep. Every year for the last decade or so."

"Is this where you gave her the ruby necklace?"

Uncle William leaned back in his chair, the memory reflected in his eyes. "I haven't thought about that necklace in years, but it seems like just yesterday." He used his napkin to wipe away a tear. "I remember the night I gave it to her. She was actually scared to open the box." He chuckled.

"She was scared? Why?"

"Well, it came in this beautiful, old, wooden case, but the carving on the lid looked just like a human ear. I thought it was strange, but I'd never paid it much attention until I gave it to Flo. Your aunt didn't like the image much. In fact, she made me keep the box, even though she kept the necklace. She loved that thing. I'm glad I picked it up when I had the chance. I sat on it for years, waiting to give it to her. Did you know that she even had a portrait made while wearing it?"

"Yeah. I think that's real cool."

When dinner was finished, Melanie followed her uncle as he wandered the restaurant, trying to orient himself as they searched the gallery of photos. Melanie rubbed her hands impatiently. When her uncle's eyes teared up, she knew he had found it. Melanie leaned in close. The photograph showed Aunt Flo as a young girl standing beside a black man who was holding a trumpet. Below the picture, a brass plate read: "JAZZ will always have a HOME in my soul." That was it. There was nothing more. *Is that the next clue?*

"Uncle William, this has been the best day ever. Thanks for bringing me."

"It was my pleasure, Mel. Today has brought back a lot of good memories. It's been way too long since I've been down here."

"Are you ready to head home? My feet are kind of starting to hurt."

Uncle William laughed. "You know what? Mine, too."

11

COURAGE UNDER FIRE

The sweet smell of maple glaze filled Melanie's kitchen. It was a beautiful Tuesday morning, and there was no better place to be. It was torture sitting there watching Ms. Arnaud prepare dinner for Mardi Gras night. Melanie's stomach rumbled loudly.

"How about a sample?" Melanie asked.

"You girls. Just like when you were little," said Sybil's mom. "You both used to sit there like puppies, beggin' for scraps."

"Mom, you're the best cook in Louisiana," said Sybil. "How could we not want licks?"

Melanie sat on a stool at the kitchen workstation, her feet dangling and a sketch pad spread out in front of her. Since coming back with Uncle William, she had filled pages and pages with designs and images. The bold colors and styles during Mardi Gras had found a place in her brain, and they would not leave until she got them down on paper. Not surprisingly, the new clue had become a kind of theme running through the book. She had written, "Jazz will always have a home in my soul," over and over again in every artistic font she cared to sketch.

Sybil sat next to Melanie, reading the newest issue of *Vibe* magazine. It had been a long time since they had both sat there. Melanie had forgotten how much fun it was to watch Ms. Arnaud concoct her recipes. A little pinch of this and a little dash of that would result in the most delectable gourmet delights. Sybil's mom hummed as she went about her business. Sybil knocked Melanie's leg with her shoe.

"Have you thought of anything new about the clue?" Sybil whispered.

Melanie laid down her pencil. "No, but it won't stop swirling around in my mind."

Sybil sighed. "Mine, too. Tell me about the picture again."

"It's just a photo of Aunt Flo with Louis Armstrong. He has one arm around her waist, and the other is holding a trumpet. The only other thing is the tag."

"Jazz will always have a home in my soul. That's gotta be the clue, but it could mean so many different things," said Sybil.

"I know. I guess it could mean we have to find some famous jazz club, but I searched all of Aunt Flo's favorites already. This was the only place with a hint of a lead."

"There has to be more to it. We're missing something." Sybil fanned her face with the magazine. "Wait, how was it written? Was everything spelled correctly, or did it look funny?"

"It seemed fine to me. Here, I wrote it down." Melanie flipped back to one of the pages in her sketchbook. She had carefully drawn out the photo's caption.

"You're right. Look's normal."

"Wait. Something is bugging me." Melanie stared at the page while tapping her pencil against the tabletop. "There was something else." She used her eraser to clear a few words and then rewrote them. "It was more like this."

Now the writing appeared different. She had capitalized the words JAZZ and HOME.

"OK, now that's something to go on," said Sybil.

They both sat and stared at the page. The longer she stared, the more the letters began to squiggle around. "It's not working. I don't get it," said Melanie.

"Well, New Orleans is the home of jazz. I don't know how to get more specific than that."

"Sure, but New Orleans can't be the answer. I just don't know."

"You girls want to try some of these cinnamon apples?" interrupted Sybil's mom. "I've shoved as many as I can into the pie already."

"Absolutely," said Melanie. She held both hands before her in a cup shape. "Lay them on me."

Soon the only sounds to be heard were the crunching of apples and Ms. Arnaud's humming. An occasional slurp sounded when juice dribbled down the girls' fingers.

"Brain food. Just what I needed," said Sybil.

Melanie agreed. "Maybe the clue has something to do with both the photo and the caption," she said between bites.

"Well, let's see," said Sybil. "Do we know exactly where the picture was taken?"

Dorine White

"Yep. Right at the bar in the restaurant. I noticed the spot when we left."

"Well, that can't be it. Are you sure there wasn't anything else there?"

"Nope, not that I could find," said Melanie. She flipped her pencil over each knuckle, back and forth like a stairway. Her thoughts drifted back to that night. "What if it means something about Armstrong's home?"

Sybil slapped her magazine down on the counter. "Maybe she means where he was born?"

"Where was he born?" asked Melanie.

"Somewhere in the slums, uptown. He was homeless for a while."

"How do we find out exactly where?"

"We could look it up on the "Net."

"Or," said Melanie, "maybe it means the Louis Armstrong museum. Isn't it built near his birthplace?"

"Totally. I've never been, but I hear they have a bunch of memorabilia and stuff."

Finally, it felt like they were onto something. "Sounds like a plan. But first..." Melanie stopped short. The smell of perfume floated into the kitchen, fully stifling the smell of spices. Only one person smelled like that.

"Melanie, are you in here?" Her mom's voice called from down the hallway.

"I'm in the kitchen, Mom."

The tap-tap of her mom's high heels sounded on the wooden floor as she approached. Each tap made Melanie uneasy, but she wasn't sure why. When her mom stepped into the room, all the air left Melanie's lungs.

The peeved squint of her mother's eyes was enough to remind Melanie that her secret best friend was sitting at the workstation.

"Melanie, a word." Her mom's voice dropped to a whisper.

"Okey-dokey." Melanie shot Sybil an apologetic look before scooting out of the kitchen. She found her mom standing in the hallway with her arms folded and foot tapping.

"What is *she* doing here?"

"Who? Sybil?" Melanie knew whom she meant, but she was feeling a bit ticked.

"You know exactly who I'm talking about. I thought we had an understanding."

Melanie slapped the wall. "That's not fair! Sybil is one of my best friends. I don't care what side of town she lives on."

"Melanie Dufour, that girl is not a good influence on you."

"My name is Melanie Belaforte! And I'm not a little girl anymore. I can pick my own friends." Three years ago, she had not been able to stand up to her mother. This time, she'd had enough. She was not going to lose Sybil again. She watched as her mother's teeth clenched.

"Melanie, you can't go around with just anybody. Everybody will judge you by who your friends are."

"Well, doesn't that sound a little obnoxious? Why should anyone care?"

"That's how life works, Melanie. Sybil doesn't go around in the same circles that you and I do. Remember when you were little? She used to get you into all sorts of trouble. What if that starts happening again? There are better people you can hang out with. People more like us."

"Mom, I'm not going to argue. Sybil is my friend, and nothing you say is going to change that."

The sigh that issued from her mother's lips was loud and dramatic. "Fine—for now. But we'll take this up again when I get back. Right now, I'm gathering things for the cruise. I need to know what I'm out of." Her mom lifted her hand to her brow to wipe away imaginary sweat. "My goodness. I can hardly remember why I came down here in the first place."

Melanie didn't say a word. She wasn't going to play her mother's game.

Rosanne cleared her throat. "Oh yes, I need to find my sun hat. I believe you borrowed it a few weeks ago when you went to the pool."

"Sure. I'll find it and drop it on your bed."

"See that you do," said her mother with a sniff. Then she turned on her heels and sauntered back down the hall. Without missing a step, she called back over her shoulder, "Oh, and please tell cook that I've changed my mind. I want a lemon pie, not apple."

Melanie dragged her feet across the kitchen floor. She felt exhausted.

"Everything OK?" asked Sybil.

"Yeah. Mom's just looking for a hat."

"What? And it's so super-secret she had to talk to you in the hall?"

"No, that's just my mom. She's twisted." Melanie glanced down at the sentence sprawled across her sketch-book. "Let's figure out a time to go. It'll have to be after Easter. Things will be easier once my mom is gone."

She looked up at the beautiful apple pie Sybil's mom was putting into the oven. Melanie groaned, "Ah, Ms. Arnaud. My mom changed her mind. She says she wants lemon instead."

The cook straightened her shoulders. "Then I guess you girls will get this one all to yourselves."

12

PICNIC DOLDRUMS

M ardi Gras had been fun, but then Melanie had to go back to school. She'd endured two weeks of classes, all the while thinking about the clue, and Easter was still weeks away. Today was the Saturday picnic her mom had arranged with the Cerisees. She was on her way upstairs when she noticed the mail on the silver tray. One of the letters seemed different. In fact, it was written with a metallic green ink. She glanced around before picking up the letter to make sure she was alone. The letter was addressed to Aunt Florence! Melanie snatched it up and stuffed it into the stretchy waistband of her pajamas.

"Melanie! What are you doing down there?" her mother called from the top of the stairs. "You're not even dressed."

"Mom, its Saturday. I slept in."

"No excuses, Mel. We're supposed to leave within the hour, and you're in your nightclothes." Her mom appeared fit to pop right on the spot.

"Give me one sec. I picked out some clothes before breakfast." Melanie flew up the stairs, careful to keep one hand on the hidden letter so it wouldn't fall out of her flannel bottoms.

Upstairs, three designer outfits lay sprawled across her bed. Melanie wavered between the white shorts with navy trim, a bold floral sundress, or designer jeans and a blouse. The terrible diva sisters didn't deserve so much of her attention, but she wouldn't skimp on fashion. She might not enjoy the picnic with her mother, but she would dress to impress regardless.

"Today is going to drag." Melanie plopped down on her bed and threw a pillow at her door. She *so* didn't want to go. She wanted to stay right where she was, alone in her bedroom. But her mother was already downstairs, probably working herself into a tizzy.

The decision was made when she considered the curious letter she'd found. She slipped into the jeans and a brightly striped blouse, stuffed the envelope into her pocket, and headed downstairs. Her mom stood by the front door, tapping her foot. She was scowling. Melanie knew she had taken too long, but she just couldn't care. Her mom ought to know the torture she was inflicting on her only child.

When they arrived at the hillside park, the Cerise family was already there. A large gazebo tent announced their lofty presence. Melanie trudged up the grass behind her smiling mother.

Large blankets and pillows covered the ground under the spacious canopy. Pierre lounged with a champagne flute in one hand. His evil daughters sat beside him.

Charity glared at Melanie, but Melanie ignored her. She glanced at Grace and caught the remains of a smirk.

"Pierre, this is truly magnificent. However did you manage?" gushed Melanie's mom.

"It was nothing a little palm-rubbing couldn't handle. Come. Take a seat," said Pierre. He held out another champagne glass. Melanie sat as far away from him as possible. Her feet hung over the edge of the blanket, onto the green grass. Despite her mother's beseeching glance, there was no way she was moving any closer.

Pierre opened a large, wicker basket, and the aroma of roasted chicken filled the air. He placed containers of food on the blanket. Melanie caught sight of ripe watermelon, homemade biscuits, and chunky potato salad. She took some time to load her plate with food, and then headed back to her chosen position.

As the conversation went on, Melanie popped food into her mouth and studied the beautiful landscape. The little park offered a lot of privacy. Small groves were arranged in strategic locations, surrounded by manicured beds of flowers and glossy evergreen bushes. The sound of running water brushed her senses. A river was close by. She relaxed as the cool breeze touched her skin, and the chirping of birds filled the trees. She had almost forgotten about everybody else, until her mother squealed.

"Oh, Pierre, you shouldn't have!"

Melanie turned quickly, dropping a bite of salad on her napkin. Pierre leaned over her mother's wrist, struggling to clasp a bracelet. From the rainbows of sparkles, Melanie guessed there were diamonds. Glancing at the Cerise girls, Melanie noticed they both had puckered eyebrows.

"It fits perfectly. Thank you, darling," said Melanie's mom.

Pierre leaned over and placed his lips against Rosanne's hand. "It's my pleasure." He peeked up at all three girls. "Why don't you girls go for a walk?"

Melanie could tell it was more than a suggestion. Disgruntled, she placed her plate aside and stood, brushing off crumbs. Her mother was gazing into Pierre's eyes, completely oblivious. Melanie sighed. She'd have no help there. Reluctantly, she followed Charity and Grace down a dirt path.

She stayed several steps behind, not wanting to join them, but it didn't seem to matter. They carried on as if she weren't there anyway, but their voices drifted back to her.

"I can't believe he just did that!"

"I know. He never gives jewelry."

"Things are getting way too serious."

"I don't like where this is leading..."

Melanie stopped walking. She did not want to hear any more. Charity and Grace strode on, their voices growing softer. A side path branched off to her right, and the sound of bubbling water met her ears. Dismayed to think she might be stuck with Charity and Grace as stepsisters, Melanie headed down the small lane. At the brook, she sat down on a rickety wooden bridge and pulled off her shoes. She let her feet dangle in the cool water, wishing she could drown her thoughts of Pierre and her mother, but she had other things to distract her. She pulled the crumpled envelope out of her jeans pocket. She opened the mysterious letter and read it silently:

Dear Florence Dufour,

My name is Sara Bogus. I am twelve years old, and I live in Ohio. This may sound a little strange, but I'm hoping you can help me with something. I am looking for a ruby necklace purchased at Baker's Antiques store in London around 1950. The only information I have is that it was sold to someone from New Orleans. When I Googled "New Orleans and ruby necklace," it sent me to a painting of you, wearing a ruby necklace. You probably already know this, but the painting is on display at the New Orleans Museum of Art. So far, it's the best lead I've found.

If your necklace is the one I'm searching for, then it came in a carved, wooden box. The etching on the lid was of an ear. If you have any information or know where the necklace is now, will you please call me? My number is 410-555-2221. I have discovered some incredible information about the ruby in the necklace.

Thank you,
Sara Bogus

Melanie read the letter twice before stuffing it back inside her pocket. *Another clue? Unbelievable.* She couldn't be sure it was the same necklace, but it seemed unlikely to be a coincidence. A letter asking about the ruby pendant had arrived just as she had begun her own quest to find it? They had to be searching for the same thing. At least it gave her a new place to search: The New Orleans Museum of Art. She sat and planned, waiting before she dragged herself back to the canopy.

Rosanne and Pierre were happily sharing food with each other, dual grins on their faces. The twins sat glowering in a corner of the canopy, whispering to each other. Melanie decided to take action. She walked right up to

her mother and sat between her and Pierre. She reached
for her mother's plate and snagged a piece of watermelon.
Then she popped it into her mouth, letting the pink juice
run down her chin. The twins giggled, and Melanie smiled,
grabbing another piece of fruit.

Rosanne cleared her throat and handed Mel a napkin,
while Pierre stood up and announced it was game time.
The giggling stopped.

∽ 13 ∾

PRIVATE EYES ARE
WATCHING YOU

T he entire week at school, Melanie felt like pulling her
hair out. She had more important things to do than
math and English. When Saturday finally rolled around,
Melanie bribed Jason with fudge brownies to take her to
Sybil's without telling her mother. She had only been to
Sybil's apartment a few times, and that was a long time ago.
Everything looked different than she remembered. The
buildings were gray and dingy, and the smells of cabbage
and spicy okra overwhelmed her senses. Jason pulled the
car over in front of an old, three-story apartment building
made of whitewashed bricks.

Melanie peered up the stairs into the dark recess where
the door to Sybil's apartment hid. Her body felt tense,
ready to flee, but she ignored those feelings and slowly

walked up the stairs. On the landing, a low-wattage bulb hung from the ceiling, its glass cover filled with dead bugs. The front door flew open before Melanie could knock.

"You found it," said Sybil. "I wasn't sure you'd really come."

"Well, it's different than I remember. It's been so long I wasn't sure I was at the right place."

Sybil gestured for her to enter. Inside, everything appeared exactly as Melanie remembered. It was as if time had stopped.

"Wow, I totally remember now," she said.

The living room of the two-bedroom apartment had vivid, orange walls with sky-blue accents. A red sofa took up most of the space, but the thing that stood out most was the humongo wooden cross hanging on the wall.

"Let's head to my room," said Sybil.

Melanie followed Sybil past the small kitchen where a large bowl of sweet potatoes sat on the table. Half were peeled, and Melanie suspected that Sybil was supposed to finish the rest.

Once in Sybil's bedroom, Melanie couldn't help but mark the differences from three years ago. Where there used to be a three-story doll house, an entertainment system, complete with a TV, DVD, and Blu-ray players, took up an entire wall. The room was no longer covered in posters of kittens and Disney characters, either. Now, images of rock bands were spread across the walls and ceilings.

"Wow, you have an awesome room."

"Thanks," said Sybil, flopping down on her bed. "So, any news?"

"You'll never guess what came in the mail. I snatched it up before Uncle William saw it. It's written to Aunt Flo, and it's about the necklace." Melanie dug the letter from her pocket, and then flattened out the crumpled paper so Sybil could read it. "It can't be a coincidence. Check it out!"

"Mel, this is great. It's like the pieces of the puzzle are coming together."

"I know, and I think we have our next move."

Sybil raised an eyebrow. "And what would that be?"

"I want to head to the museum and find that painting of Aunt Flo."

"Hmm. I think there is a bus line that runs right by there. We can Google it."

"I can do us one better," said Melanie. "Jason is parked just outside your neighborhood. He can take us. Do you think we'll have time to head down there today?" It was already nearing two o'clock.

Sybil squirmed, her shoulders slumping. "I wish. I still have a few chores left."

"What if I helped? Could we make it?"

Sybil jumped up. "Yes! I'll go get the vacuum. You finish peeling the sweet potatoes. They're in the kitchen."

Melanie called Jason and told him their plan. Then, working together, the girls finished up the chores. In no time, they were on their way, confident that they would make it to the museum with time to spare before it closed.

As they approached the museum, Melanie felt its majestic presence. On each side of the museum were large, stone urns. Above them, Greek bas-reliefs reminded Melanie of the Parthenon. Stairs led up to Greek columns guarding the entrance to the massive building. Large banners hung on either side of the door, announcing an exhibit of French Impressionist Edgar Degas's work.

"Where do you think the painting would be?" asked Sybil. "This place has tons of side galleries."

"I don't know. Let's ask someone."

"Wait, there's a map," said Sybil. Inside, the girls grabbed a brochure and began walking. All around them, people studied different artworks and sculptures. Melanie unfolded the pamphlet and scanned the list of galleries.

"Our best bet is probably the Louisiana art section. It says here that they have an outstanding survey of Louisiana art from the nineteenth and twentieth centuries, many pieces donated by generous Louisiana families."

"Perfect," said Sybil. "Which way?"

"We have to go through the European art section first. Then wind our way to the modern art, and then the local art."

The girls walked past several tourist groups and entered the French gallery.

"Oh my!" said Melanie. "Look at that painting."

Prominently displayed on the far wall was an enormous picture of a French woman dressed in a sapphire-blue dress, sitting on a red settee. "It's gorgeous." The woman's hair looked like a white bird's nest, and a large blue hat with feathers sat on top. "My mom would love that hat, but I don't think she could pull it off."

"The placard says it is Marie Antoinette. Wow. Isn't she the one that said, 'Let them eat cake'?" asked Sybil.

"Yep. I think she got her head cut off."

"Eeew. Come on. Let's keep going. The museum closes in an hour."

Sybil took the lead this time, charging through different salons. Melanie wasn't as fast. She stopped in front of a bronze sculpture of a ballerina. Entranced by its beauty, she started when Sybil tugged on her shirt. "Come on, Mel. Make time for Degas later."

They finally made it into the Louisiana section and stopped before a picture of the old museum, then known as the Delgado Museum.

"Who was Delgado?" asked Sybil.

Melanie leaned closer to the picture, focusing on the small print. "Says Isaac Delgado offered funds back around 1911 to create 'a temple of art, for the rich and poor alike.' It made Louisiana a major hub for the arts back then."

"Cool. Let's find the local displays."

Melanie found the painting of Aunt Florence right next to a jumbo, patchwork quilt displayed like a tapestry. In the portrait, the ruby necklace hung around her aunt's neck, its beauty and brilliance somehow captured by the artist. Melanie stared. It was eerie to see Aunt Flo in the museum. It was almost like seeing a ghost.

"Psst. Sybil. Over here."

When Sybil joined her, Melanie stepped closer, wanting to take in the painting more thoroughly. It had been painted long before madness had confined her aunt to the house. In the painting, Aunt Flo's cheeks were rosy and her eyes glowed with life. The ruby necklace hung from a silver chain against her aunt's pale skin. The ruby itself was at least an inch long and oval shaped, surrounded by delicate filigree.

Melanie turned to Sybil. "Now we know what it looks like."

"What? You didn't remember before?"

"Not clearly. I was just a kid. Hey, wait!" Melanie turned back to the painting, and then took a step to her left. "Did you see that?"

"See what?"

"The eyes," whispered Melanie. "They blinked, and look. Now they're following me." Melanie took several steps to the left, hiding behind an artistic rendering of a windmill with a man riding flying elephants. Aunt's Flo's eyes followed her every step.

"Mel, I don't see anything. It's probably just one of those optical illusions."

"Why can't you see it? She's totally looking at me."

"Maybe I'm just standing in the wrong spot. Walk toward me while I look at the picture."

Melanie marched toward Sybil, focused and determined not to look at the painting as she moved.

When Sybil's mouth fell open, Melanie stopped and then whispered. "You saw it too, didn't you?"

Sybil nodded, but her eyes didn't leave the painting. "It only follows you. Nobody else."

Melanie took a few steps backward, putting distance between herself and the portrait. As she did so, a ghostly arm emerged from the painting, pointing her way.

Sybil screamed and then threw herself in front of Melanie as if she was a living shield. Melanie grabbed her friend's shoulders, gripping them tightly. Both girls began backing up one step at a time.

"Why do they always point at me?"

"What do you mean?" asked Sybil.

"The one in the crypt did the same thing."

"What! What one in the crypt?"

Melanie peeked over her shoulder, scouting their path for artwork. "I didn't tell you."

"Best friend, here. Why not?"

"I convinced myself it was the heat."

"Mel!"

"Sorry! I'll make it up to you. Promise."

"Oh yes you will!"

"At least this one doesn't make me feel like I want to pee my pants. I'm not getting the soul-stealing vibe like the last one had." Melanie looked at the painting again.

One of the eyes winked at her, and then the arm withdrew into the painting.

Melanie stumbled backward, almost tripping over her own feet. "We're going too slow. Let's get out of here."

Melanie grabbed Sybil and headed out to the sculpture gardens. Outside the sky had dimmed as evening approached, but there was enough daylight left to take in the immense gardens, small lakes, and beautiful, bronze sculptures. Melanie stopped in front of a large, red, modern piece that spelled LOVE.

"You seem to be a magnet for weird lately," said Sybil.

"Tell me about it. We'd better get back before we get in trouble. My mom's not going to be happy if she gets home before I do and figures out we spent time together."

Sybil froze.

Oops, totally wrong thing to say. "I'm sorry, Syb, but you know what I mean."

"Yeah, I do, and it's not cool. I'm going home."

14

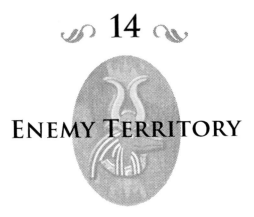

ENEMY TERRITORY

Finally, spring break arrived. Melanie made a point of hanging out with Sybil the entire first day. Just before she left, she pulled from her pocket a gold bracelet that had belonged to her grandmother.

"Sybil, this is for you. I want you to know that you're my best friend."

Sybil held the bracelet in her hand, fingering the dainty heart locket that swung from the chain. She wrapped Melanie in a fierce hug. "You're my best friend, too."

Later, the day after Easter dinner with her family, Melanie was shipped off to Pierre's house. She hoped her mother had a really nice cruise, because Melanie was the one truly paying for it. Pierre Cerise's house was everything Melanie imagined it would be. It stood tall, with large columns and a gigantic front porch. They'd eaten dinner in a grand dining hall with chandeliers and a polished, cherry dining set. The room Melanie occupied was beautiful. Satin covered everything. It wouldn't have been such a terrible place to stay if Grace and Charity didn't have rooms right down the hallway.

That first night, it was after eleven before Melanie was ready for sleep. When she'd entered the guest room, a light shone through the window, illuminating her way to the bed. She didn't bother with the overhead light. Looking back, that would have saved her a lot of trouble.

Halfway to the bed, she heard a small croaking sound—inside the room. Her eyes focused on the window, opened just a crack. *Darn*, she thought. *Something got in.* She felt too tired to care, and flopped down on the bed with a splat. That's when everything broke loose.

Not just one croak, but dozens filled the air. The blanket on her bed began to move, then out popped a frog, and another, and then another. Soon she had frogs hopping all over her body. Some became tangled in her hair. All of them let out frightened croaks, but Melanie's screams drowned out the amphibians' sounds. Fast as lightning, her door flew open. Pierre stood there with slippers on his feet and a robe barely tied about his waist.

"Melanie! What is it? What's wrong?" he yelled. With a flick of the switch, the overhead light turned on, and Melanie didn't need to say a thing. Frogs flew across the room with determined leaps. Her blanket looked as if it were giving birth, as frog after frog struggled to find the way out from under it. Pierre stood with his mouth wide open. Melanie would have giggled, but she was still desperately trying to untangle a frog from her hair.

Glancing past Pierre, Melanie saw the twins lurking in the shadows, their bodies doubled over in laughter. Melanie's face turned deep red.

"Don't worry, Melanie. We'll have things cleaned up in a moment." Pierre seemed oblivious to his daughters' laughter behind him. "I'll wake up the housekeeper, and we'll have those frogs out in a jiffy."

After ripping the stuck frog out of her hair, Melanie turned her back on the devious twins.

"I'll talk to the staff about leaving the windows open. This won't happen again," said Pierre, and he hurried off.

Melanie finally got to sleep a little after midnight. All the frogs were gone—at least, she hoped they were. Her bedding was new, and the window was firmly closed.

The next day, Pierre wanted to spend time with all three girls. He took Melanie and the twins to lunch and then to the movies. Grace and Charity texted the entire time. They ate lunch with a fork in one hand and their phones in the other. Plus, they barely said one word to Melanie. *Argh*.

Pierre tried to fill the silence with chitchat. Melanie could tell that he was working exceptionally hard to make a good impression. He actually was not a disagreeable guy. As they walked out of the theater, he glanced back at the twins and sighed.

"You're a teenager. You know how it goes," he mumbled.

Sure, thought Melanie. *Only I'm not being rude and ignoring everybody.*

That night when Melanie went to bed, she checked her sheets for unwelcome guests. Beautiful, crisp linen was all she found, and she happily sank into bed.

At 2:00 a.m., however, she sprang up from the bed, her hair a mess, and her heart bursting. An alarm clock was honking, full blast, somewhere in her room. With a shriek, she ran around, checking every corner and drawer. *Where is that coming from?* She couldn't find it. The loud *EE-EE-EE* sound grated on her eardrums, making her want to shove her head under her pillow. It was no use. There was no way she'd get back to sleep unless she turned off that alarm.

After fifteen minutes of stumbling about, she finally found the offensive weapon tucked under her dresser. She felt like beating the clock against the wall, but that wouldn't really solve anything. So she simply hit the off button, and dumped the alarm into the trash can.

Come morning, Melanie had a headache, and all she wanted was some peace and quiet. Luckily, the twins had piano lessons that morning, so she wouldn't have to deal with them for a while. After a thirty-minute hot shower, Mel was ready for some Sybil time.

Pierre had his driver pick up Sybil, and together they sat on Melanie's lush guest bed. The plan was to visit the New Orleans Jazz Museum at the old Mint building—the museum had several rooms accorded to Louis Armstrong—but first, a little payback. Melanie had a plan. She led Sybil along the hallway and stood silently in front of the twins' bedroom door. There was no going back now. Melanie shoved the door open and took a step into enemy territory.

The room was enormous. Two twin beds covered with pillows were the main focal points, but every single item—from the curtains, to the pillow shams, to the dust ruffles—was color-coordinated in teal and purple. Melanie wondered if they had done it themselves or used an interior decorator.

"Wow!" said Sybil. "It's like a whole other world in here."

"Sure, if you like that kind of stuff. To me it screams, 'We have no style of our own.'"

Sybil laughed. "Either that or 'We're so totally spoiled rotten.'"

"Let's spread out and find some dirt," said Melanie.

The girls took off in opposite directions. The plan was to find some incriminating evidence in order to humiliate the twins. They left no stone unturned, but they found nothing. The entire room was perfect. The only personality present was in the CD rack, but even though Melanie didn't share their taste in music, it was not enough to bring them down.

About to leave in disgust, Melanie noticed two forgotten items: the girls' school packs tucked behind the door.

"Hmm," said Melanie.

She unzipped one while Sybil took the other. Typical school stuff filled both bags. *Darn!* thought Melanie. Then her hand brushed a spiral notebook at the very bottom. Raised writing rolled under her fingertips.

When she pulled out the notebook, Melanie saw the prize staring back at her. Hearts and kisses in goopy glitter-glue covered the entire notebook, but the largest heart, front and center, had a story to tell. In big, puffy letters were the words "Charity and Sean." On the bottom of the page, Charity had written "Mrs. Sean Melbourne" in swirly letters.

"This is perfect!" said Melanie.

"Who is Sean?" asked Sybil.

"Only the top-ranked soccer player at New Orleans Prep."

"Is he Charity's boyfriend?"

"Nope, and that's why this is so perfect." Melanie hugged the notebook to her chest. "We know Charity's big secret. She's in love with Sean!"

"So?" asked Sybil.

"So! Let's give their room a heart attack."

"A what?"

"You'll see. Let's go find some construction paper, pens, and tape."

One hour later, Melanie and Sybil rested in the center of a pile of paper hearts, all decorated with love notes to Sean.

"Now we just have to tape them all around the room and voila, a heart attack."

"Nice," said Sybil. "I never would have thought of it."

Mission accomplished, the two friends started on their second assignment of the day. They jumped on a streetcar and headed to Uptown New Orleans, where they purchased their tickets for the Jazz Museum and waited in line for the tour. The building itself was modest, but inside it screamed jazz. Trumpets and cornets hung everywhere they looked. Larger-than-life posters showed Louis Armstrong performing in places such as the Cotton Club, the Waldorf-Astoria's Empire Room, and Hollywood, California.

Part of the museum documented Armstrong's life from his birth in poverty, to living in a home for boys, to his travels in Chicago, Los Angeles, and New York. Melanie was surprised to find that he actually hadn't spent much time in New Orleans.

They followed the guide through a room devoted wholly to Armstrong's Grammy Hall of Fame records. The speakers played scratchy recordings of his trumpet playing and raspy vocals.

Then they came to the room they had been waiting for, the personal effects room, a veritable treasure trove of knickknacks that had once belonged to the king of jazz. The tour guide left the group alone. People browsed the personal property, and several shopped at the gift store. Melanie and Sybil carefully examined each and every item in the room. Luckily, many rested on tables and in cabinets. Only a few valuable items were locked behind glass.

Each item had a small sign next to it explaining its importance to Armstrong. Long after the last of their tour group left, the two girls continued inspecting the room. Soon another tour group came in, busily talking and taking pictures.

"Psst. Sybil, over here."

Sybil joined Melanie beside a round table. Displayed on the tablecloth were objects that had been donated to the museum. Melanie pointed to a small bud vase. It stood barely six inches high and had a large, bulbous bottom and a narrow neck. Deep-blue glaze covered the porcelain. Right next to it, a card read, "Bud vase celebrating the blues—a gift to the museum from prominent New Orleans resident Florence Dufour."

"This is it. This is the clue," whispered Melanie.

"OK, but what does it mean?"

"I don't know, but it must mean something."

They stood in front of the table staring at the miniature flower vase. Melanie was at a loss for an explanation. Only one thought kept running through her mind: *I need that vase.* Her heart pounded, and she felt the blood rush into her ears. Just as the next tour group entered, she grabbed the vase and tucked it inside her jacket. With all the noise and talking, no one noticed except Sybil.

Melanie speedily left the room through the gift shop, trying not to look too conspicuous. Sybil followed close on her heels. They didn't stop walking until they were halfway down the street. When they did, Melanie couldn't help looking back for fear of pursuers.

"Now that took some guts," said Sybil.

"I can't believe I just did that," answered Melanie, panting.

"Well, let's take a look at it."

Melanie slowly uncovered the vase. Something inside rattled. "I think there's something in it."

"What?"

Melanie held the vase up, trying to look into the tiny neck. "It's no good. I can't see a thing."

"Here. Let me try." Sybil aimed the vase toward the sun. "Darn, the glaze is too thick."

"That means we're going to have to break it open."

"Not here. Let's get away from the scene of the crime," Sybil said, pulling Melanie down the road toward the nearest streetcar.

They rode back to the Cerisees' home in silence. Melanie gripped the vase tightly, unaware that her knuckles had turned white. Once there, they sneaked around to the back garden, out of sight of anyone in the house.

"I really hate to do this," said Melanie.

"We don't have another choice," said Sybil, shrugging.

Melanie took a deep breath and then shattered the vase on a rock. Pieces flew everywhere, cluttering the pathway. Melanie dropped to her knees, her hand reaching out toward the mess. A silver chain wove itself among the broken pottery. She cleared the path of broken shards, following the thin, shiny links into the grass. Nestled among the short, tender stalks was a glint of red.

She picked up the silver chain, allowing the smooth, oval stone to swing in the air. The ruby was a deep and beautiful cherry-red. Its facets reflected crimson sunlight onto Melanie's hands.

"Holy moly!" said Melanie. She hesitated, her fingers trembling as she reached out to touch the glistening gemstone. It was so beautiful. But when she finally touched the ruby, an incredible pain, like a massive electric shock, flashed through her fingers, and she flew to the ground with a thud.

"What happened? Are you all right?" Sybil ran to her side.

"Don't touch it! It shocked me." Melanie reached out and picked up a twig. Crawling back to the pendant, she carefully placed the stick under the silver chain and lifted the necklace into the air. It dangled hypnotically. A red fire burned within its depths. She didn't mean to touch it again, but something about the red glow enthralled her. Before she knew it, her fingers were again grasping the ruby.

"Melanie!" Sybil shouted.

Melanie blinked, letting the gemstone go when she noticed her fingers wrapped around it. "Nothing happened this time. Wow, I didn't even realize I was reaching for it again."

Melanie lifted the necklace off the twig and held it in front of her eyes. While biting her lip, she slipped the links over her head. The ruby rested like lead on her chest. She glanced up at Sybil, thinking all was well.

The horrible, stabbing pain struck without warning right between her eyebrows. Then noise filled her ears, and the pressure in her head felt as if she were in the middle of a tornado. She gripped her temples, screaming in agony.

"Melanie! What is it? What's wrong?" Sybil grabbed Melanie, pulling her up.

Melanie raised her eyes to meet Sybil's, but glanced away when she noticed something in the bushes. Her friendly ghost was making an appearance. Its hazy form took shape, floating above the shrubs. Melanie tried to focus while her brain was being ice-picked. She squeezed Sybil's hand in a death grip. This time, the shape wasn't as indistinct as before. It kept growing sharper and more defined.

When Melanie recognized the ghost, she covered her mouth with her hands. Aunt Florence, regal and eerily majestic, floated before her.

"Well, it's about time," the ghost exclaimed.

Then, everything went black. Pain ruled the world as Melanie's body crumpled to the ground.

15

QUEEN OF THE NILE

Melanie floated in the hazy, gray nothingness of the unconscious. She couldn't feel her body. Time passed strangely, sometimes speeding up, and other times dragging on and on and on... Sometimes she'd dream that she heard voices, and more than once she saw a bright light ahead.

"Is she going to be OK?" A voice worked its way through the fog. She tried to place it. She knew it was familiar, but nothing came to her.

"I've given her a strong sedative. It should knock her out long enough for the migraine to go away."

"What could have caused such a severe reaction?" the familiar voice asked.

"We can't know for certain until we do a CAT scan. For now, I think it's a good idea to let her rest. Has her family been contacted?"

"Yes, I called her uncle. Her mother just left on a cruise. I've put a call through to the ship, but it only left the other day. I don't think she'll make it back for a while."

"Well, Pierre, she should be fine. I got here fast."

Pierre, thought Melanie. An image came to mind of her mother and a tall, handsome man. *He sounds awfully worried.*

Melanie struggled to stay conscious, but her thoughts wandered and blurred. She found herself in a long, dark tunnel with a dim light at the end. As she searched around, fear stabbed at her heart. This was not the bright light she had seen earlier. She ran her hand along the curved side of the dirt tunnel. Her fingers ran over rough patches of earth, and she felt mud caking under her fingernails. She stopped and glanced back, but there was only darkness. *What do I do?*

"I guess there's nowhere to go but forward," said Melanie, trying to give herself a boost of courage.

Melanie took a hesitant step, not wanting to go one way or the other. With one foot moving, it was easier to take the next step. The tunnel went on and on, but at one point, it began sloping downward. It was a gradual change, but she could tell by the way the pebbles rolled that she was delving deeper into the ground.

She was in a dark tunnel, heading down into the depths of the earth. She tried not to think about what it all could mean. She recited the Hail Mary, but that didn't help. On she walked. The light in the tunnel grew brighter. Somewhere in front of her, something was shining. She picked up her pace until she was sprinting toward the light.

Water. It was faint, but she could hear a rush of moving currents. She burst out of the tunnel into a large, underground cavern. The air smelled rich and felt moist. Her spirits rose. Overhead, stalactites dripped down from the ceiling. The cavern looked like the inside of a cathedral.

Ahead, light bounced off the crests of a fast-moving river and reflected on surrounding rocks. She jogged toward it, wondering what she would find.

An old, wooden dock rose out of the shallows. Its wood was warped, and its pillars crooked. She stopped at the very edge, looking for something—anything—to explain where she was. The water ran steadily, dark and deep. She glanced to her right to see where the river led, but all she could make out was darkness. She had hit a dead end.

Melanie sat down and swung her feet over the rapids. Every now and then, a wave would hit the pier and splash cold water onto her toes.

"OK, time for a reality check." Her words echoed in the vast cavern.

"This can't be real. The last thing I remember, I was with Sybil in the garden, and...the ruby pendant!" Melanie reached beneath her shirt. The necklace rested safely against her flesh.

Then her memory went fuzzy. She vaguely remembered thinking about Aunt Flo, and then her head hurting. Melanie twisted the sterling chain between her fingers, struggling to remember.

"I think I remember a doctor."

THUD.

Melanie looked up but couldn't see a thing.

THUD.

The sound repeated. She gazed down into the torrential waters, afraid of what she would find. The river moved along as quickly and fiercely as before. She raised her eyes and caught a glimpse of something in the far distance, floating along the river.

THUD.

This time Melanie felt the vibration in her bones.

At the edge of her vision, a long, pointed shape poked out of the darkness. As it drew nearer, it widened into a wooden prow that sliced through the dark water. Oars poked out of the sides, dipping into the water, propelling the boat forward.

THUD.

This time, Melanie recognized a drum keeping time for the oarsmen.

The boat drew nearer and nearer, the deep vibrations shaking Melanie to the core. She began to edge her way back along the dock, keeping a close eye on the approaching boat. It moved quickly, like smoke on the water, and pulled up to the pier before Melanie could run away.

Melanie froze, not daring to take another step. The boat in front of her was long and curved, taking up the length of the wharf. Elaborate carvings and bold paint decorated the boat, and fresh garlands of flowers hung from the sides. A black cat prowled the railing. Seated upon a large, raised throne was a beautiful woman, her short, raven-black hair framing a deeply tanned face. Around her, fanning the air with large, ostrich feathers, were women dressed in white. A blush rose to Melanie's cheeks when she noticed that the seated woman wore only a thin shift. She averted her eyes and focused on the necklace hanging around the woman's swanlike neck. The necklace was gold, but there were five empty loops.

"Finally," said the woman. "Someone with some sense has my ruby."

Melanie fingered her treasure.

"You there! Girl, what is your name?" The woman's deep voice rolled across the water.

"Me? Well, umm, Melanie."

"Welummmelanie," said the woman. "I am Cleopatra, queen of Egypt and the Lower Nile."

Melanie's mouth dropped open. "But...but you're dead."

The queen's rich laughter rang out. "Of course, dear child. Come closer."

Melanie took small steps toward the ship, making her way to its side. She put a hand on the craft, hoping to be allowed on board, but a host of guards darted at her, pointing sharp spears at her chest. The queen called out, "Foolish child. Would you join me in death?"

Melanie trembled as she stepped back. "But I—"

"This ship rests on the river of death. One step onto this boat and your ba and ka would separate." The black cat wound itself around Cleopatra's slim legs. When it stopped, it turned its emerald-green eyes on Melanie and shook its head, as if it understood the queen's remarks.

"What?" Melanie backed up, wondering at the crazy queen and her cat.

"Your life force would flee your body."

"Oh," said Melanie, still confused. "So, what do you want with me?"

"You wear the ruby. I need it back."

"What? You want my ruby?" Melanie put her hand over the gem, hiding it from Cleopatra's eyes. "I went through a lot to get this thing."

"Child, before it was yours, it was mine. It is part of a set. Five gemstones that I need returned."

"But you're dead. Why would you need them?"

"I sail the river of Duat, unwilling to confront Ma'at until my gems are returned."

"Ma'at?"

"The goddess of balance, of truth. Ma'at will decide my future—whether I will see paradise or the inside of Ammit's belly."

"I don't know who Ammit is, but yuck. Here, you can have it." Melanie struggled to lift the chain over her neck, but it barely budged. She pulled harder, but she could not get it above her chin.

Cleopatra smiled at her in condolence. "The time is not yet."

The deep beat of the drum made Melanie jump.

"I cannot stay long in one place. Osiris urges me ever on to his kingdom. You must use the ruby to find the others."

The drummer picked up the tempo, and the boat began to move. "What are you talking about?"

The rear of the boat flew past the pier. Cleopatra's voice floated back on the air, "Find the others and unite them with my Ba."

Melanie watched the angry current suck the boat toward the far end of the tunnel. The beat of the drum faded. She stood there, unmoving.

"Well, great! That was real helpful." Melanie closed her eyes and shook her head. "I think I need Google."

"Melanie, sweetheart. Wake up." Uncle William's voice sank into her subconscious. She tried, she honestly did, but her eyelids wouldn't even flutter.

16

AUNT FLO, THE FRIENDLY GHOST

"Your mom called." Uncle William's voice was soothing as he spoke to his niece. "She says she loves you. I told her we would contact her if things got worse."

Melanie's thoughts focused on her mom. *Why isn't she here?* Melanie remembered something about a cruise, and then she felt herself floating away again. This time, a bright light blinded her.

"Turn down the light," Melanie demanded.

"Wow, just as feisty as I remember."

The brightness dimmed, and a figure floated in front of Melanie.

"Aunt Flo?"

"The one and only."

"But what's going on? Am I dead?"

"Nope. You're just in a state of in-between. That doctor gave you some strong stuff."

"What's happening?"

"Now, that's a good question, and one I've been waiting a long time to answer."

Her aunt gestured to Melanie's left, and a comfy sofa appeared amid the billows of white fog.

"Let's sit down. This floating takes a lot of energy."

"Please, help me. I feel like I'm going crazy."

"Oh, sweetie. I know that feeling well."

"Sorry, Aunt Flo, I didn't mean anything by that." Melanie sagged into the sofa, half-afraid she'd fall through it.

"I know you didn't, dear. Let's see. Where to start?" Her aunt pointed to the ruby pendant hanging around Melanie's neck. "The necklace, then."

Her aunt sat, neatly tucking her dress under her legs. Melanie almost laughed. Even in death, Aunt Flo was a fashionista.

"I don't know everything. I wish I'd figured it out when I was alive, but all the voices...I just didn't know what to think. That's why I've been waiting for you. I don't want it to happen again."

Melanie held up the necklace. "So, what does the necklace do?"

"It's not the necklace. It's the ruby. It conducts people's thoughts. They just come to you, like they're being shouted right into your head."

"Voices?"

"Yes. But that's not all. It also allows you to hear spirits that have not moved on. It's why we can speak now."

Melanie pointed a finger at her aunt. "It was you. The ghost was you all along!"

"Of course, dear. Who did you think it was?"

"I don't know. It was all too weird."

"Before, all I could do was vaguely appear. But now that you have the ruby, we can talk, and I can keep my shape in focus."

"All this because of the ruby? It doesn't happen to belong to Cleopatra, by any chance?"

"Why, yes, it does. How did you know?"

"I had a little visit."

"Interesting. I always knew the ruby was special, but I didn't find out anything about it until after I died. What it did, where it came from, to whom it belonged...Those little tidbits might have been useful, if I'd been in control enough to use them. That's why I had to stay here. You need someone to guide you, and who would be better than your crazy, old aunt? It's amazing how clear things are when you're looking from the other side." Aunt Flo floated back and forth, as if she were pacing.

Melanie reached out a hand to stop her. "Thank you, so much. This whole thing has been awful. When those men broke into my room, I almost gave up."

"It'll be all right, Mel. I'm right here."

Melanie tried to take the necklace off and hand it to her aunt, but just like before, she could only lift it a few inches. "Why can't I take it off?" she asked.

"It is impressing its powers upon you. It'll come off when it's ready. You just have to wait."

"Great." Melanie dropped the necklace back on her chest.

"In the meantime, you need to control its powers or you'll be in for a bumpy ride."

"How do I do that?"

"Do you remember the pain you felt when you put on the necklace?"

Melanie winced. "It was horrible. I don't remember anything else but the pain."

"Yes, it was unavoidable. You were hearing the minds of all the people around you. It can crush you if you're not careful. I was fortunate, I think, to hear voices before I had the necklace. I only got a mild headache when I first wore it."

"What do I do?" Melanie threw up her hands in despair.

"You need to learn to shield your mind. I've been thinking about it, and you need to find someone who can teach you meditation. You need to build up your walls."

"OK, I can do that. Then what?"

"Then we'll work on reaching out to hear only what specific people are thinking. I'm sure I don't know half of what the ruby can do."

Melanie suddenly felt a violent tug. Her body lifted into the air and flew backward. "Aunt Flo! What's happening?" Melanie screamed.

"Your body is sucking your spirit back. Don't fight it, Mel. You don't want to be trapped in limbo."

Pain reentered Melanie's world. First, she felt her skin come alive. It burned and itched like fire ants were swarming all over her body. Next, her heart slammed back into her chest. For a few minutes, it was all she could hear. *Thump, thump. Thump, thump.*

Then—a voice.

"Melanie, can you hear me?" asked Uncle William.

She moaned. Her skull was filled with pressure, threatening to pop like a zit. She threw her hands to her head in agony.

"Bring some more medicine. She's in pain," her uncle yelled.

Melanie heard quick footsteps. She felt a needle poke her arm, followed by a sudden rush of warmth. Then everything went fuzzy again, but she didn't float into limbo this time. She just fell into a painless sleep.

When she awoke, it was dark. She still felt a stabbing pain behind her eyes, but this time she knew she wasn't dying. Everything was quiet. *Night*, she thought. *People are sleeping.* It was then that she realized she was still in the Cerisees' guest bedroom. *Have I been here the whole time?*

She took a few moments, slowly bending each finger and toe. When she was sure that everything was in working order, she focused on the pressure in her head. She remembered what her aunt had said about building walls, so she imagined an old castle. She placed herself in the middle of it and began adding stones, one at a time. Deliberately and carefully, she focused on sealing herself inside. After a time, the pressure became bearable, and she drifted back to sleep. The next morning brought trouble. When Melanie opened her eyes, two police officers stood at the foot of her bed. One was fat and beady-eyed, and the other was tall with extra-large feet. Pierre stood off to the side, pieces of a broken vase in his hands. *Oh no!*

"Melanie Belaforte," said the first cop, "we'd like to have a word with you."

There was nothing she could do. She groaned as their mental voices wormed into her skull. *Why would she do it? Does she know we caught her on tape? Kids today.*

She couldn't deny it. Pierre held the proof in his hands. But maybe she could soften the blow. It was time to get creative.

"Melanie, were you at the jazz museum yesterday?" Fat Cop asked.

"Yes." She wouldn't give any details until she got her story straight.

"Did you take something from the museum? Maybe a flower vase?" asked Big Feet.

"Well, I guess so. It was more of an accident."

"Exactly how was it an accident?" continued Big Feet.

"I was actually just looking at it. My Aunt Flo's name was on the label. I just stood there thinking about her, and the next thing I knew the vase was in my hands, and I was out the door. I don't know why I did it." Melanie pinched herself sharply under the covers. A tear welled up in her eye.

Pierre gazed at Melanie in sympathy. *Poor girl,* his thought shot into her brain.

"That doesn't explain why you shattered the vase into bits," said Fat Cop.

"That was an accident, too. I didn't mean to drop it, but I had this horrible headache. The next thing I remember, I was here in bed, and Uncle William was at my side."

"It's true," said Pierre. "It's what I was telling you earlier. The doctor thinks it was a sudden-onset migraine."

"I see. But, accident or not, you still took something that did not belong to you and vandalized it. The law does not look kindly on these sorts of juvenile crimes," said Fat Cop.

"I'm terribly sorry, officers. I've never done anything like that before. I promise it won't happen again," said Melanie.

Big Feet looked at her with compassion. "I can tell you've had a rough time of it. We'll contact the museum and see if they intend to press charges. The vase was actually on loan from your aunt's estate. So in a roundabout way, you took something that already belonged to your family."

"But stealing is stealing," Fat Cop growled, his thoughts dark.

Big Feet winked at her. "I'll see what I can do, but something tells me you might have some community service in your future."

Melanie fell back onto her pillow. Thoughts from all three men flew at her like bullets. Plus, she could hear the twins down the hall trifling about which clothes to wear for the day. "I don't feel so well. Pierre, can I have some more medicine?"

Pierre rushed to her side. "Of course." He turned to the cops. "You'll have to excuse us. The doctor wants Melanie to take it easy. You'll need to come back later if you have more questions."

Melanie didn't bother to watch the officers leave. She focused all her thoughts on building the castle walls between herself and everyone else. It took a long time, and the pain kept hitting her in waves. She finally reached a level where the pain was bearable, but she knew she would need to find someone to help her control all the incoming thoughts. Pierre came back into the room and handed her a glass of water and two pills. She swallowed them. Fifteen minutes later, she felt the blissful, fuzzy-brain feeling coming on. Sleep came quickly after that.

17

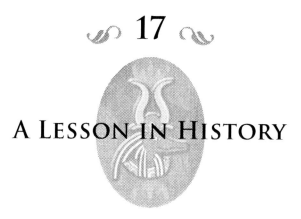

A LESSON IN HISTORY

Uncle William, Sybil, and even Jason came by to visit, but they didn't stay long, and it was kind of a relief when they left. They felt sorry for her, and Melanie didn't know what to do about it.

That night, she decided she'd had enough solitude, and it was time to rejoin the living. She made her way down to dinner on unsteady feet. Pierre and the twins sat enjoying their evening meal. Pierre beamed when she entered the room.

"Melanie, it's so good to see you up and about. How are you feeling tonight?"

Melanie sat down in her seat. Neither Charity nor Grace said hello. "My head is killing me, but I didn't want to be in my room any longer."

"Good, good." Pierre signaled to a server. "I'll have them bring you some hot soup right away. It'll make you feel better."

Melanie doubted it, but nodded her thanks. She ate her soup in silence.

Charity leaned over and whispered in Melanie's ear. "It was you, wasn't it?"

"Me, what?" asked Melanie.

"You plastered the room with hearts. You found out about Sean."

"So?"

"Well, you'd better not tell anyone, or else."

"I think you've got that backward," said Melanie. "You'd better stop picking on me, or I will tell."

Charity puckered her lips and then glanced away, defeated. Grace stuck her tongue out at Melanie and then turned away too.

After dinner, Melanie went back to her room, feeling jollier than she had since finding the ruby necklace. Nighttime was the best time. Most of the people were gone, and those who stayed were watching TV or zoning out. The stress on her skull dropped at least 75 percent.

The only problem was the spirits. She'd started noticing them after her headache had eased up. They didn't have a sense of time and would pass through her room as if they were out taking a stroll. At any time of the day or night, she'd hear them talking, mostly about previous lives, and then they'd wander away. Melanie guessed it was the ruby drawing them into her presence. But if they knew she could hear them, they would stick to her like glue, wanting her to fix their unsettled business. She did her best to ignore them.

Now she knew how Aunt Flo had felt.

Tonight she pulled out her laptop and decided to do some research. Over the last couple of days, she'd been thinking about what Cleopatra had said. She was confused about a lot of things. What in the world was the Duat? And what did ba and ka mean? They sounded like the sounds a dying animal would make.

Unfortunately, the idea of getting information was easier than actually finding it. There was so much stuff on ancient Egypt that Melanie had to refine her search several times. Finally, she ended up on an article about the afterlife. The first thing she saw was a picture of a bird with a human head. This was the image of the ba. As far as Melanie could tell, the ba represented the soul. More than that, it represented everything that made a person unique or gave him or her personality.

The ka was different. It looked like an image of two arms raised into the air. Melanie found out that it was the spirit, or the vital essence, of a person. It was the part that brought life to the soul and distinguished whether a person was dead or alive. If the ka left a body, that person died. *Wow*, thought Melanie. *Glad I didn't get into that boat.*

Melanie clicked on the name "Osiris," and up popped an image of a green man with a black, pointy beard and a big, tall hat with feathers. Mummy wrappings covered his feet, and in his hands, he held the Egyptian crock and flail. To Melanie, they looked like a scepter and a hook, but for the Egyptians they were the symbol of the pharaoh. Next to his name in bold print it read, "God of the dead and guardian of the gates of paradise."

Further on, the word Duat was highlighted, so she clicked the link. A stunning print came up, a drawing from the Egyptian *Book of the Dead*. On the papyrus, Melanie could see a large throne with a figure sitting on top. In front of him rested a scale with a feather placed in the middle. At the base of the scale sat the craziest creature Melanie had ever seen. It looked like a lion, but it had a big butt and the face of a crocodile.

Melanie read the caption. The scene represented the weighing of the heart in the Duat, or underworld. If your heart didn't measure up, Ammit, the devourer, aka the crazy creature, ate it. *Hmm. I don't think I'd want to meet that beast. No wonder Cleopatra was worried.*

Melanie pushed her laptop away.

"Jeez, not a cheery thing to look forward to."

"Yeah, tell me about it."

"What?" said Melanie. When she glanced up, she knew she'd made a mistake. There was nobody else in the room.

"You can hear me!" shouted a voice.

"Keep it down. I just got over my last headache." Melanie lay back against her pillow, waiting to hear what this particular spirit wanted from her.

"I can't believe it. Praise the gods. I knew I felt the presence of a powerful Egyptian priest."

Melanie could tell from the voice that the spirit was a man, or used to be, but she couldn't see him. "Just tell me what you want. I've got things to do."

"Well, aren't you in a hurry? I've been wandering around for the last couple thousand years, and you're in a hurry."

"Sorry. It's just that there are a lot of spirits out there, and they all want something."

"Well, I won't keep you. Not if you help me."

"What do you need?" Melanie felt wary. She couldn't imagine how she could help such an ancient spirit. Would she even know what he wanted her to fix?

"When I died, the priest didn't perform the opening of the mouth right, and my ba was unable to leave my body."

"What does that mean?"

"The opening of the mouth is performed to allow us to eat and drink in the afterlife. I need you to say the correct words so my soul, ba, can be released and join with my spirit, ka. I want to become an Akh."

"A what?"

"An Akh. For an Egyptian, it means a complete entity. I know all the words from the *Book of the Dead* and can easily pass through the Duat. I just need my ba released. Please, will you do it?"

"I just need to say the words? Nothing else? No blood or gross stuff?"

An eerie laugh echoed through the room. "No. You just need to say the words from my Coffin Text."

"But I can't speak Egyptian."

"The answer to that is easy." The spirit hovered behind Melanie and then shot forward, straight into her body. Melanie jumped around the room, swatting at her body and flinging herself around in an awkward dance.

"Get out!"

"Calm yourself. I can't take control of you. Just open your mouth."

When Melanie realized that she was in complete control, she calmed and opened her mouth. Out flowed the spirit's words with precision and correct pronunciation.

When she spoke the last word properly, an immense sigh blew through her mind. "Thank you, dear one." And she knew the spirit was gone.

Melanie stared down at the ruby hanging around her neck. What other powers did it hold? Could she use the powers to help other people? Melanie was beginning to think of the ruby in a new light.

⁓ 18 ⌁

A FEW CALM BREATHS

Two days later, Melanie sat on a red woven rug in the middle of Cecile's store. It had taken her that long to convince her uncle and Pierre that she was OK to leave the Cerisees' house, and that was only after the CAT scan at the hospital had come back clean. There were so many people and spirits in the hospital, Melanie thought she might go insane. Their screams of pain echoed in her head. She had acted like a deaf mute so that the various spirits would not know she could hear them.

"I'm glad you came to me Melanie. I can sense turmoil boiling around you like a storm. The spirits are in an uproar," said Cecile.

Melanie eyed the voodoo priestess. "Tell me about it. You should hear all the stuff they keep yelling."

Cecile looked at Melanie in distress, "You mean you can actually hear the dead?"

"Yep. Dead and living." Melanie held up her ruby necklace to show Cecile.

The woman cringed and backed away, her hands waving before her. "Put it away. Put it away! It's blinding."

Melanie looked down at the ruby in her hands, it looked the same to her, but still she tucked it under her shirt.

"Goodness. I haven't seen anything give off that much spiritual vibration in my life. It's like a living inferno."

"It's why I'm here. I didn't know where else to go. I mean, I don't think anybody but you and Sybil would believe me."

Sybil looked up from the stool she balanced on, and then went back to examining a bunch of unusual ingredients.

Cecile bobbed her head in agreement. "Among the people you know anyway. First, are the spirits troubling you now?"

"Yes, but mostly it's all the people walking in the streets outside. They're all thinking different things, it's like there's a tornado in my brain."

"Here," said Cecile. "Let's try this." Cecile grabbed a bag from one of her counter tops and then spread white chalk around Melanie in a large circle.

Instantly the voices stopped, and the tension left Melanie's skull. "What did you do?"

"I just made a protection circle. It'll only help while you're in it, and I doubt you want to spend the rest of your days sitting on my floor. So, what were you thinking I could help you with?"

"Well, I need to learn to meditate, to block out the voices of both the dead and the living."

"Yes. Well, let's begin with the basics," said Cecile.

Melanie spent a dull thirty minutes learning about breathing techniques and aromas. Cecile walked around her waving a burning stick of lavender. The smoke circled around Melanie, and she breathed it deeply into her lungs.

"Good, it's working already. Deep, steady breathing," said Cecile.

Melanie struggled to let her body relax. It wasn't easy. Slowly, over time she began to focus on the sound of her own heart beat and breathing.

"Yes. I can feel your peace," said Cecile.

Melanie startled for a second when she felt Cecile uncurl her left hand and dropped something small and hard into it.

"Shh. Relax," said Cecile. "The item in your hand is a stone, one of the most basic elements on earth. A stone has no other purpose than to be a stone. It is strong and unyielding. It takes hundreds of years just to smooth away its surface. It is a rock."

Melanie wrapped her fingers around the stone. It felt cool to her touch. Part of the stone was smooth, yet the bottom seemed bumpy and coarse. An image came to her mind of the stone laying in a creek bed, water washing around it.

"Now Melanie, I want you to be the stone."

"Hmm?" said Melanie.

"Be the stone. Imagine yourself hard as a rock and tough as nails."

Melanie tried, but she couldn't grasp the idea. She kept picturing herself trapped in a rock, like a chick in an egg. Her unbalance worked its way from her thoughts to her actions, and soon her heart began to race like an engine.

When she opened her eyes, she saw Cecile nodding at her, a small smile on her face. "Don't worry Melanie. Rome wasn't built in a day. You need to practice."

"I guess it couldn't be easy."

Cecile laughed, deep and rich. "Nothing in life ever is." Cecile turned towards Sybil. "Sybil put that down!"

Sybil dropped a pile of what looked like small dried bones unto the counter. *Wow*, thought Melanie. *She's got eyes in the back of her head.*

Cecile returned her attention to Melanie. "A castle wall is made of stone, but it often tumbles down. You need to be the stone itself, the thing that remains after all the centuries of wear and tear."

Melanie squeezed the rock tight. It felt solid and real, unbreakable. She thought about Cecile's words and slowly nodded. "I get it. I'll practice every day."

"More than once a day," said Cecile. "Any free time you find, focus on your breathing and then become a rock. Soon it will be second nature to you and the voices will come only when you want them."

"Thank you Cecile." Melanie struggled to her feet. Her legs felt heavy. She'd sat in the same position for too long, and her muscles protested the movement. She handed the stone to Cecile.

"No, you keep it. Carry it around in your pocket. It'll help you remember to practice every time you feel it."

Sybil hopped off her stool. "So, we going?"

"Yep, we going." smiled Melanie. "Just let me put my I-pod on, it helped block the voices on the way down."

19

A MOTHER'S LOVE

That night, the carpet brushed against Melanie's bare feet as she padded down the hallway. She hated having to go to the bathroom in the middle of the night. Her footsteps automatically slowed as she passed the twins' room. It was silly. It was well past midnight, and they were probably asleep. But as Melanie passed by their door, she heard something.

She couldn't help herself. With her ear pressed against the door, she held her breath and listened. On the other side, she could hear a quiet, sniffling sound. It sounded as if someone was crying. Then she heard a quiet voice. "Shhh, Charity. It's all right."

Melanie listened, pulling her hand away from the doorknob.

"I miss her. I want her back."

"I know, Charity. I miss her too."

"It's not fair. She wasn't supposed to die. She was supposed to see us grow up."

"I know. She was supposed to show us how to put on makeup. Teach us how to pick the perfect outfit. Tell us how to meet boys," said Grace.

"Yeah, she was going to teach us to crochet, remember?"

"I do."

More sniffles came through the door, and the twins' thoughts of sadness crashed into Melanie.

Melanie stepped backward. She was not sure what to make of the sudden turn of emotions in the twins. They always seemed so mean and cold...

A voice spoke out of the darkness. "My poor, poor babies."

Melanie spun around. The hall was empty behind her.

The voice spoke again, this time louder. "You heard me, didn't you? You can hear me!"

Melanie froze.

"Oh, this is wonderful. After all these years. Someone can hear me."

It took a moment after being so startled, but Melanie quickly realized, *This is my chance. I can use the ruby's power to help this spirit.* Melanie gestured toward the origin of the voice. "Shhh! Follow me." Melanie headed back to her room.

Inside her room, Melanie plopped down on her bed and crossed her legs.

"OK. Let's start with who you are. And what do you need?"

A feminine voice answered from somewhere in front of Melanie. "After all this time, I can't believe it. My name is Polly Cerise. This is my home."

Melanie took several moments to digest this new info. "So, you are Charity and Grace's mom?"

"Yes. My poor babies."

Those girls are anything but poor, thought Melanie. "Why are you still here?"

"I can't move on. Not until they have the albums. They need to know how much I love them."

"Do you mean that if I help you, you can go on to heaven?"

"That's right. It has been so terrible watching them and not being able to tell them. When I went to the hospital I didn't have time to get them out of the trunk, and, well, then I had other things to worry about."

"You mean their baby albums?"

"They have their baby stuff, but they don't have my letters. I had several months to prepare, so I wrote each of them letters. You know, for special occasions—their first date, sweet sixteen, marriage...I tried to think of everything. I just wanted them to have something special from me. Little things, really. Pieces of advice, my thoughts, and wishes. My love, bound and delivered, for them to carry throughout their lives."

Melanie got off the bed and paced the room. Her feet worked a trail in the plush carpet. She hated the twins, didn't she? They had done some awful stuff to her, but now she felt really badly. Melanie could not imagine a life without her mom. How would she feel in their position? Maybe she'd misjudged them. She remembered hearing the twins crying in their room earlier, and her heart twanged. Sure, they were not best friends, but this was their mom! Of course, she was going to help. *This is why the pendant came to me.*

"Can you tell me where the letters are?"

"Oh, yes. They're in my crochet trunk. After I died, Pierre couldn't bear the thought of seeing it every day. He moved it into one of the storage rooms. He never knew about the letters. I didn't tell him about them because he always insisted that I was going to live, that somehow my cancer would be cured. He refused to talk about any other possibility, but then it happened so fast. The albums of letters are under the afghans. Will you help me?"

"OK, I'll get the books and give them to your girls. Will you be all right after that?"

Instead of a response, Melanie heard soft crying.

"Can you tell me what the trunk looks like and where the storage room is?"

Sniffle. "It is an old, oak trunk. Its lid is decoupaged with violets. The storage room is downstairs beside the kitchen. It's just a small, walk-in closet."

"OK. Here I go." Melanie headed for the door. "I'll see what I can find."

Once again in the hallway, Melanie tiptoed toward the stairs. She wasn't sure why she felt the need for silence, but it seemed appropriate—sneaking around somebody else's house in the middle of the night.

The kitchen was easy to find. The closet door off in the corner appeared old and rickety, and it squeaked when she opened it. A single light bulb hung from the ceiling. Melanie switched it on by pulling a string. Boxes and junk crammed the room. She slowly turned in a circle, examining everything in view. The oak chest was easy to find, but it rested under a few boxes labeled "books."

By the time Melanie had moved the heavy boxes, beads of sweat clung to her forehead. She took a second to rest before opening the trunk. Inside, beautiful crocheted blankets lay folded in neat, little piles. She carefully moved them out of the chest, placing them on a spot on the floor that wasn't dusty. At the very bottom of the trunk, she uncovered two leather-bound books. They were square and bigger than normal notebooks, more like oversized portfolios.

After pulling out the books, she wrapped each one in an afghan and refilled the chest with the remaining blankets. Her job now done, she returned to her room.

The room was silent. She had no way of knowing if the ghost was still there. So she cleared her throat.

"Excuse me. Ms. Cerise, are you still here?"

She waited for several tense seconds before an answer came.

"Oh, you found them. Thank goodness. You are such a sweet girl. Please, go give them to the twins. Tell them how much I love them."

"Don't you want to tell them yourself?"

"No, dear, that time has passed. Just give them the letters, and then they'll know."

"OK, but they'll wonder where I found them."

"You can tell them what you wish." A gasp exploded. "Do you see it? Do you see the light?"

Melanie looked all around, but the room seemed exactly the same. "I think the light is for you. Maybe you should follow it."

"It is so warm. I can see people waving at me. Oh! One is my Grandma Prudence. Grandma! Wait, I'm coming."

The room fell quiet. Melanie waited a few moments more before whispering, "Are you still there?"

Silence.

"Great. Now I have to deal with the evil twins."

Down the hall she went. She could still hear whispering behind their door, but it sounded softer. She tapped the door with her knuckles.

No answer.

She knocked again, a little louder. This time, the door swung open, and Grace shoved her head out into the hallway.

"What do you want?"

Melanie bit back her natural response. "Can I come in?" she said as she struggled to balance the books inside their blankets.

Grace snorted, but curious, she moved aside to let Melanie pass.

Charity sat on a window seat. Her eyes narrowed as Melanie entered.

"I have something for you," said Melanie.

"What could you possibly have that we would want?" demanded Charity.

"Yeah, we don't do our shopping at Goodwill," hissed Grace.

"You know what? You two suck. You're mean and spiteful, and I can't believe I felt sorry for you." Melanie dropped the books onto the floor. The blankets surrounding them puffed up to reveal the treasures beneath. "Here," she hollered. "These are for you." Then she turned on her heel and left, slamming the door for good measure.

Back in her room, Melanie fumed. Doing something nice and sending someone to heaven was great, but the fact that she had helped Grace and Charity made her want to puke. She threw back her covers and jumped into bed.

Twenty minutes later, an unexpected tap brought her out of her twilight.

"What!" Melanie was not about to get out of bed for them.

The door cracked open, and in poked Charity's head. "Where did you get these?"

"Why should I tell you?"

Charity came into the room. Grace followed. Both girls gripped their albums to their chests. The moonlight coming through the window allowed Melanie to see tears running down their faces. She gave a massive sigh.

"You wouldn't believe me if I told you."

The twins came forward slowly. They stopped beside the bed and then sat on her comforter. Melanie had to move her legs to give them room.

"Do you know what these are?" Grace asked.

Melanie debated her answer. "Well, I didn't look through them, but I thought they were albums."

Charity bobbed her head. "They're our books. Letters mom wrote to us before she died." She wiped her nose with her sleeve and then sniffed.

Totally not ladylike, thought Melanie.

"Thank you for giving them to us," said Grace. "They mean more than you could ever know."

"Well, if you owe me, maybe you could tell me why you hate me so much?" asked Melanie. The twins were in a giving mood. Maybe she could get some answers.

Charity looked at Grace. They both shrugged at the same time.

Grace continued. "It's your mom."

"My mom?" asked Melanie.

"Yeah. Dad has us. He doesn't need anybody else," said Charity.

"You guys have been mean to me for years. Our parents only started dating a couple months ago," said Melanie.

"Shows how much you know," said Grace, smugness creeping back into her tone.

"Yeah, your mom and our dad have been making eyes at each other for years. We could only hold our dad off for so long. He finally decided we were old enough for him to start dating again. Ugh!" said Charity.

"Are you kidding me? You've been a pain all this time just because you don't want our parents to date?" said Melanie.

"It's not just dating," said Grace. "He has every intention of marriage, and we do not need another mom. Our mom was perfect!"

"Look, I don't want to be related to you any more than you do, but don't you think you should let your dad have a choice here?"

"NO!" both girls yelled in unison.

"Um. OK, but can you stop taking it out on me? I gave you the books, remember?"

The twins gazed down at their albums and then up at each other. "Deal." Charity seemed reluctant to agree, but Grace, at least, seemed genuinely sincere and grateful.

Melanie felt a wave of warmth in her chest. Helping the spirit had felt good, and now maybe Charity and Grace would cut her some slack. She hoped they'd remember not to hate her, in any case.

It was only after the twins left that Melanie remembered that she still hadn't made it to the bathroom. With a grunt, she swung her legs over the bed and headed for the hallway.

20

A Thief in the Night

M elanie sat cross-legged in her own backyard. It was so nice to be home finally. She closed her eyes and concentrated on her breathing. Cecile had been right. The more she practiced her meditation, the easier it became. She could slip into her "rock" mode after a few quick breaths. Life felt manageable now—at least she felt sure that she wouldn't have to cringe the next time she walked into a room full of people. She was grateful, however, that she had some time before she'd have to test that theory. There was one more week of spring break.

Melanie wondered if things would be any different now that she and the twins had a mini truce. Oh well. She'd have to wait and see, but she'd know soon enough—she could read everyone's thoughts, after all. She still hadn't decided if that was a good thing or a bad thing, but what choice did she have?

The ruby felt smooth between her fingers. Every day she had tried to lift it off, but so far, she'd only managed to raise it off her chest a few inches.

"Don't worry. It'll happen soon enough."

Melanie jumped. "What? Who's there?"

"Turn around."

Aunt Flo hovered near the rose bushes in a vain attempt to smell their sweet fragrances.

"Hi, Aunt Flo," said Melanie. "What are you doing here?"

The ghost floated across the grass until she landed a few feet in front of Melanie. "I just have this feeling... something really bad is about to happen."

Melanie laughed. "I didn't know ghosts had feelings."

"Really funny, little missy. Just 'cause I'm dead doesn't mean...Oh, never mind. Now then, things have been buzzing up here in the afterlife. All of a sudden, there is a lot of chatter going around about your necklace."

"Why would ghosts be talking about me?"

"I'm still trying to figure that out, but there seems to be a certain group of spirits focused only on you. They're truly strange, all with a ghastly tattoo of a pyramid on their shoulders."

"How does a ghost get a tattoo?"

"The tattoo is a remnant from their mortal lives. It must have meant something deeply significant to them for it to appear on their spirit bodies."

A flash of a pyramid tattoo ran through Melanie's brain. It seemed familiar, and then she remembered the ghoul in the tomb.

"Aunt Flo, I think I've met one of the ghosts before." Melanie bit her lip hard as she fought off the feeling of panic sprouting in her mind like a weed.

"Oh dear! Do you still have the gris-gris bag?" asked Aunt Flo.

"Yeah. I shoved it into a drawer."

"Well, put it under your pillow. It'll help keep the evil spirits away, for now. I don't like how focused they are."

"Will it keep you away, too?"

"No, just spirits that mean to do you harm. It's not the voodoo so much as the effort that went into making the bag. It's filled with positive energy."

"OK, I'll do it tonight."

"No, do it as soon as possible. I just can't shake this feeling."

Melanie lifted herself from the ground, flexing her knees. "Sure thing, Aunt Flo. Enough weird stuff is happening around here. I'll do it now."

"Good girl. I'll keep exploring things over here. You be careful." The ghostly body of Aunt Flo dissolved until it was nothing more than wisps of smoke blowing in the breeze. Melanie headed inside.

That night, she dreamed. The breeze blew against her skin as she pumped her feet harder and harder. She caught air, and then shot back onto the seat of the blue, rubber swing. When the swing reached its apex, she could see everything in the park in front of her. A little dog yipped at its human, tangling its leash around its owner's legs. The man went down, all splayed out like a pancake. Melanie couldn't stop her giggles.

As the swing flew backward, she closed her eyes, smelled the fresh grass, and felt the warm air. It was a beautiful day. It almost seemed that she could reach up into the blue sky and touch the fluffy clouds.

She watched a little boy riding his scooter in circles. Around he went on the asphalt, enough times to make

Melanie dizzy. A mom pushed a baby in a stroller along the cement path bordering the park. Melanie could see the baby's chubby, little hands gripping the cushioned sides.

Everything was glorious. In fact, Melanie decided she would swing forever. She clutched the chains tighter in her hands and pumped faster. She would go so high that she would soar. But then something went wrong.

The chains turned in her grip. She slowed herself down to control them, but they kept twisting in her palms. Melanie dragged her feet in the dirt, trying to stop her momentum. Her arms yanked at their sockets as she tried to pull herself off the seat. Her feet hit the ground, but then the chains wrapped themselves around her wrists and would not let go.

Her face broke out in a cold sweat as she struggled, but the chains were strong. She reached up high, trying to loosen their grip. Instead, the chains twined around her neck and tightened, the links digging into her skin. She couldn't breathe.

Suddenly, she felt her body rise off the ground and then slam straight down. She awoke with a jolt, and when she opened her eyes, reality hit.

Someone was on top of her, wrestling with the ruby necklace. Strong hands twisted and pulled, choking her. She gasped for air. It was dark enough that Melanie couldn't see the attacker, but from the weight on top of her and the strength of the hands, she guessed it was a man. Melanie flailed her feet like windmill blades. It didn't help. The attacker only pushed harder.

She grabbed the necklace chain to pull it away from her throat. Sweet air rushed into her lungs. Then the villain's hands were back. If Melanie could speak, she would have told him it was no use. *The necklace won't come off!* But she doubted that he would listen.

The edges of her vision began to darken, and she came to a grim realization: if she were dead, the necklace probably would come off. *He's going to kill me!* She fought harder. The man's face came into view as moonlight beamed through the window. *Jason!*

Jason was leaning over her, choking her with his bare hands. *Why is Jason doing this? He works for my uncle. He's a friend.* As his face drew closer to hers, his alcoholic breath filled her nostrils. She felt lucky for a little air, but then he clamped down tighter. Without thought, she reacted. Thrusting her hands out, she dug her thumbs into the fleshy parts of his eyes. The solid orbs of his eyeballs pressed back, but she didn't let up. She shoved with all her strength.

With a grunt, Jason rolled off her body, covering his eyes with his hands. She took the chance to scramble off the bed. Jason was between Melanie and the door, so she headed for the window. She only made it a few steps before he lunged forward and pulled her feet out from under her. Melanie went down with a bone-jarring crash, and the air gushed from her lungs, preventing a scream. Jason's hands clung to her ankles in a viselike grip that Melanie couldn't break.

Ignoring the pain in her throat and knees, she rose onto her elbows and began to crawl. Jason held tight, pulling her back toward him. It was a desperate tug of war. For every inch she gained, he pulled back two. Instinct took over, and she began to kick, hoping to hit anything. He stopped pulling as her kicks became more violent. Then she scored a lucky hit. She felt her heel crash into his chin, connecting with bone.

His hold on her loosened, and she half crawled, half stumbled to the window. With a quick thrust, she threw it open. Instantly an ear-splitting alarm shrieked through the air. Thank goodness her uncle had updated their security system.

She fell onto the floor in a lump, both hands wrapped around her raw throat. She struggled to force a scream out, but her vocal chords were bruised and felt like sandpaper. Jason took one step toward her, and then raised his fist in the air. *This isn't over.* His thoughts lanced through Melanie's brain. Then he turned and took off. Melanie could hear his feet pounding down the stairs.

She lay on the floor, the security alarm still blaring, until Uncle William and the house guard appeared in the doorway and switched on the lights. Her uncle gave her one look before flying to her side. She struggled to speak, to tell him about Jason, but her throat wouldn't work. The security guard took in the scene and then sprinted off, looking for the intruder.

"Melanie! Melanie! Talk to me. What happened?" Her uncle rocked her back and forth in his arms.

Soft footsteps raced into the room. Melanie peeked up to see the horrified face of her mother. She reached her hand toward her mom, desperate to feel her touch. Her mother joined their little huddle on the floor.

Melanie saw one of the live-in staff run into the room, her hands trembling as she grasped her terry-cloth robe closed.

Uncle William turned. "Quickly, call the police and then get some water."

Melanie didn't move, happy to let everyone take care of her. When the water came, it flowed down her throat in welcome relief. She had to try a few words before her voice came out audibly.

"Mom. Uncle William."

"What happened?" asked her mom.

"It was Jason. Jason attacked me."

"What?" bellowed her uncle. His face turned as red as a radish, and he jumped to his feet. "How dare he!"

"Oh, my baby," cooed her mom.

Melanie shakily pulled out the ruby pendant from under her nightgown.

Uncle William gasped and staggered back. His lips moved silently as recognition dawned.

"Oh, Melanie. Where did you find it?" Rosanne asked, bewildered.

Melanie watched her uncle, afraid he would have a heart attack. She needed to tell the truth—just not the whole truth. "Remember that vase I broke?"

"The one from the jazz museum?" asked her mom.

"Yes," said Melanie. "When it broke, I found the necklace. It must have slipped off Aunt Flo's neck somehow and found its way inside the bud vase before she gave it to the Armstrong museum."

Her mother clutched Melanie to her chest. "Why didn't you tell us?"

"I was in so much trouble already, and then I got sick. I was afraid to tell Uncle William, and you weren't back from your cruise."

Uncle William eased himself down onto Melanie's bed. "I don't know what to say." A ruckus sounded in the hallway. "It must be the police. I'll take care of things." He got up to leave.

"They're going to want to talk to me, aren't they?" said Melanie.

"Yes, dear. You just tell them what you told us," said her mom. "They've heard stranger things than a servant trying to rob his employer."

"That piece of filth. If I ever see him again, I'll kill him myself," raged Uncle William.

"William, make sure they send up a paramedic. I want them to look at Melanie's neck."

Her uncle went out to bring back the reinforcements. Melanie could vaguely hear the commotion of their thoughts as she tried to erect her emotional wall.

"Mom, I love you."

"I love you, too, dear. Just relax. William will take care of everything. He's good that way."

"Mom, I want to call Dad."

Melanie felt her mom's arms drop to the floor. "Are you sure?"

"Mom, just because I want to call Dad doesn't mean I don't need you too."

Air rushed through her mother's lips, blowing Melanie's hair out into wisps. "I know, dear."

21

COMMUNITY SERVICE

The home intrusion didn't put her community service on hold. The next day, Melanie pulled on canvas gloves and trudged over to her group. She grabbed a black garbage bag in one hand and a poker in the other. Her community service hours had begun, and spring break wasn't even over yet. *Ugh.* The judge had sentenced her to twenty-five hours of community service just for breaking Aunt Flo's vase. She wouldn't have a free weekend for months.

After the attack, her uncle had tried to get her out of her court-mandated community time, but the judge wouldn't budge. The decision had been made while she was still recovering, which was just as well. She hadn't been in any condition to be around large groups of people. To pass the time, she decided to practice hearing individual thoughts. Everywhere she looked, she was surrounded by other kids in overalls, all assigned to pick up garbage along Louisiana Route 99.

Of all the kids around her, she felt the strongest urge to tune in to the guy with the pierced lip, nose, tongue, and eyebrow. She focused solely on him. At first, it was difficult, blocking out the incessant chatter of everybody else's thoughts. But after a bit, she figured out how to zero in on him and only him. It was excellent practice. He was older and buffer than the rest of them, but he had spent some major time in juvie, and his thoughts overflowed with remembered violence.

Next, Melanie zeroed in on a girl with pink, spiked hair and ripped-up stockings. Her thoughts revolved around missing her little sister and wondering when she would have time to text her boyfriend. Melanie decided to see if she could get the girl talking.

"Hey, have you done this before?" asked Melanie.

Maybe if I ignore her, she'll stop talking, thought the girl.

Melanie snorted but tried again.

"My name is Melanie. What's yours?"

Debbie, but out popped, "Zing."

"Zing. Cool name. Did your parent's name you that?"

"My parentals are dead. The name's my own." However, Melanie clearly heard, *I miss them. Wonder if they'll take me back?*

"Nice tattoo on your arm. Do you have more?"

"Sure, tons." *Fat chance! Not after this one. Hurt like crud.*

Melanie tried not to laugh, but it was hard. "Hey, do you know enough about the tattoo scene to recognize a tattoo if you saw it?"

"Depends what the tat is."

"What about a pyramid with a scarab beetle crawling on it?"

Zing spit. "Yep, I know that one. Total scabs. They showed up in town several months ago, talking all fancy, offering money for info."

"What kind of info?"

"How should I know? I'm not a narc."

Melanie could tell from the silence in the girl's mind that she didn't know anymore. "But, there was more than one?"

"Think so. Maybe three. Why you asking?"

"Nothing. Just thinking about getting a tattoo. But something original. I want something nobody else has."

"Whatever." *Tattoo my butt. That girl has high society written all over her. No way would she do it.*

How does she know where I'm from? Melanie wondered. *We're all in work clothes. I'm not even wearing makeup.*

Melanie blocked her telepathy after that and put on her headphones.

Picking up trash was monotonous. *I can't believe I'm here doing this.* The day dragged on, long and hot. It hadn't taken long for her to fall into a rhythm—she stopped thinking and automatically moved from pile to pile. While she was lost in this funk, a white van zoomed down the street toward her. She couldn't hear a thing over her music, so when the car screeched to a stop on the road beside her, she didn't notice.

When rough hands grabbed her shoulders and pulled her off the ground, however, she yelped. Her head and shoulders were already inside the van before she could really react. Luckily, the punk with the body piercings moved fast. He swung his poker straight at the guy holding her, bashing the kidnapper's head. Melanie heard a grunt and managed to flip her body around to fight him off.

"Let go of her!" the pierced boy yelled as he grabbed Melanie's overalls and yanked her backward. A tug of war commenced as the kidnapper struggled to pull Melanie into the van. Her arms felt as though they would pop out of their sockets as they were pulled in different directions. She let out scream after scream, desperately trying to escape. From the corner of her eye, she saw the supervising officer running their way, but he was at the other end of the street. While the kidnapper pulled at her shirt, she dragged her fingernails up his arms, leaving trails of blood. She felt chunks of skin curl under her fingernails and tried not to retch. She reached up and grabbed the man's shirt, trying to pull it over his head as she had seen hockey players do, but he still didn't released his grip.

Freaking kids! the man thought. *Let the girl go. She's mine.* He gave Melanie another tug, trying to rip her from the hold of the boy. She felt her rescuer's grip loosen and heard the kidnapper think, *finally*, just before she heard the blessed cock of a gun.

"Let go of the girl or I'll shoot," yelled their security officer.

Several foul words shot into Melanie's brain, some in a language she didn't even know, but the meanings were clear. Melanie fell to the ground, and the van zipped away, the side door sliding shut with a bang. As she landed, tangled up with her rescuer, she accidentally clipped his nose ring with her elbow.

"Sorry," she said as she righted herself, her head exploding as all the people on the highway turned their thoughts to her and the incident they'd just witnessed.

"Are you two OK?" the security officer asked, panting. The boy with the body piercings rubbed his nose while smiling up at the cop.

"This mean we're done early?" the boy asked.

Melanie just lay there, stunned.

"You two sit tight. I'll call for some help. When they get here, they'll want to ask you some questions. Melanie Belaforte?" he said, pointing her way. "I'll call your emergency contact and have them come pick you up. Do you need an ambulance?"

Melanie shook her head, not trusting herself to speak yet. Tears welled up in her eyes as she thought about what might have happened.

She sat on the curb, trying to work through her deep-breathing exercises. It was a little rough with the other kid pacing next to her, but she closed her eyes and tried to make it all just go away. She only glanced up when a black boot kicked her tennis shoe. Fat Cop and Big Feet Cop glared down at her. *Oh great.*

22

THE EMERALD RING MAKES AN APPEARANCE

U ncle William's feet traced the same path over and over on the living room carpet. His cheeks purple, he repeated the same sentence over and over.

"How dare they!"

Sitting on the sofa, Melanie could only watch as he worked out his anger. Melanie's mom sat to her right, holding Mel's hand in a firm grasp. A wadded up piece of tissue rested in her other hand, and occasionally her mom would dab at the corners of her eyes.

"The new security system is not enough. As of this moment, Melanie will have her own bodyguard," said William.

Melanie jumped to her feet. "Are you kidding me? What am I going to do with a bodyguard?"

Uncle William pointed his long finger at her. "An attempt on your life is no little matter. I don't understand it. The ruby necklace isn't worth kidnapping you for. Maybe they really are after a ransom."

Her mother tsk-tsked. She stood and smoothed out her dress. Her tissue fell unnoticed to the floor. "I think a bodyguard is a good idea. William, will you see to it?"

"Definitely. In the meantime, Melanie, you are not to leave this house. I'll call the lawyer and get your community service postponed."

"Fine." Melanie flopped back down on the sofa. She hoped he found someone soon. She didn't like being bottled up at the house, not that she felt like leaving at that moment.

Two days passed in absolute boredom. They wouldn't even let her go to church, they were so worried. Melanie watched TV, surfed the Net, and even attempted to clean her room. It was while collecting her dirty laundry that a forgotten letter fell to the floor. She bent over to pick it up, remembering it had mentioned the ruby necklace. Just then, Melanie's phone buzzed. She looked to see who was calling, and saw Sybil's number. The text message read "He."

What? thought Melanie. *She must have butt-dialed me.* She put the phone away. Then she unfolded the paper and reread the letter.

"I wonder who Sara Bogus is and what she knows about the ruby?" Melanie grabbed her cell and dialed the number on the paper. As the phone rang, she sat down on her bed, only to jump right up when a girl's voice answered the phone.

"Hello?"

Melanie took a deep breath. "Hello, is this Sara Bogus?"

The voice on the other end hesitated, but then answered, "Yes, who's calling?"

"This is Melanie Belaforte. I live in New Orleans." Excitement bubbled in Melanie's chest. She had to move and wandered over to the window.

"Did you say New Orleans?"

"Yes. Florence Dufour was my aunt. I got a letter from you about a ruby necklace."

Melanie had to hold the phone away from her ear as the girl on the other end began whooping and hollering. It took time for the girl to calm down. Melanie tapped her fingers against the windowpane, waiting. She wanted some answers and she had a feeling this excited girl had some.

"Why do you want to know about the necklace?" asked Melanie.

"First off, do you have it or know where it is?" questioned Sara.

"Yes and yes. It's right here, stuck to my neck."

"Oh, you've put it on," said Sara. "By any chance did anything weird happen?"

"You could say that," answered Melanie. "Why?"

"It's a long story, and it will be hard to believe if you haven't experienced it firsthand."

"Try me. Weird is my new middle name." Melanie leaned her forehead against the cool glass.

"OK, I'll just tell you my story. Then, if you've had something similar happen, you can tell me yours."

"That sounds fair."

"Well, it all started with an emerald ring."

"An emerald?" Melanie broke in.

"Yep, an emerald. I'll get to the ruby in a sec. Anyway, when I put the ring on, it got stuck on my finger."

"Stuck!" Melanie grabbed her necklace and gave it a good yank. *Yep, still stuck.*

"Yes, hold on. I'll tell you the story. It turned out that the emerald in the ring did some freaky stuff." Melanie heard Sara take a deep breath, and then the story spilled out fast. "I suddenly started hearing animals, what they were saying. Then I turned into an Egyptian cat. It was scary, and then there were these dreams about Cleopatra."

Melanie sat down on the floor, her legs trembling. "You saw Cleopatra, too?"

"Well, I dreamed about her, but I can't say I actually saw her. Wait, did you see her?"

"Yes, I, um, well...I had a visit from the queen herself."

"Oh, my goodness! You are definitely the one," said Sara.

"The one what? And what does the ruby have to do with all this?"

"OK, see, Cleopatra had five magic gemstones. They all had different powers, though I only know what two of them do. Anyway, she separated them from her necklace and sent them off before she died so that the Romans wouldn't get them. The only original clue I had about the emerald was that it had a partner in a similarly carved box at the jewelry store: a ruby pendant."

"My ruby!"

"Yes! Claire—she's the woman who owns the antiques store in London—she told me the ruby was sold to someone from New Orleans. It was sheer luck that your aunt had her portrait done wearing the necklace. It came up when I Googled New Orleans."

"Wow, that's amazing." Melanie leaned her head back against the wall. Her hands shook as she held the phone.

"Tell me," asked Sara, "does the ruby make strange things happen?"

"Oh, yeah, and I know you'll believe me, too." Were there things Sara could tell her that she didn't want to know? She couldn't believe she was telling all this to a total stranger. "It lets me hear other people's thoughts, and if there are any ghosts around, I can talk to them."

"You're kidding. That's great, and don't worry about the pendant sticking. It'll come off once your body is in balance with the magic. I learned that the hard way."

"Sara, is that why you wanted to find the ruby? Just to see what it could do?"

"I wish that was it, but I'm afraid there's bad news, too."

"Of course. Out with it."

"Unfortunately, the Romans are still after Cleopatra's five gemstones."

"What? The Roman Empire died out hundreds of years ago. Do you mean the Italians want the gems?"

"Nope. These are descendants of the actual Roman soldiers that were alive at the time of Cleopatra. Their sole purpose in life is to recover the gemstones and use their powers to take control of the world. And we don't want that. Trust me."

"These...these people. Did they come after you?" Melanie rubbed her neck, remembering how Jason had almost strangled her.

"Yes, that's another reason I was hoping you'd call. These people are members of a cult, an extremely dangerous cult. They'll stop at nothing, not even murder, to get the gems."

"That's what I was afraid of."

"Then you've met them? You'll notice they have a tattoo on their bodies of a pyramid and a scarab beetle."

Melanie banged her head back against the wall. "That stupid tattoo! The guy who tried to get me at the cemetery had that tattoo, and the guy in the van! Oh wait, and the ghosts, too..."

"Melanie, you need to be very careful. You can't let those guys get the ruby."

"Believe me, I know. But I have to tell you, when I spoke to Cleopatra she said I needed to find all the missing gems and return them to her."

"What? But I only know where one other is."

"Cleopatra told me to use the ruby to find them. I just haven't mastered the gem yet. I'm still at the beginning stages."

"We need to keep in touch. I have this friend named Kainu. He's got Cleopatra's onyx. We'll need to work together and find the other two."

"Look, I've got to go," said Melanie. "This is a lot of info to take in. Let's connect on Facebook, and I'll call you if anything more happens."

Carefully flipping her phone shut, Melanie rose from the floor and stared out the double-paned glass. It seemed strange that outside the window things were beautiful and sunny, the earth bursting with spring; while inside, she was so full of dread. She was in the dark, scared, and unsure. *What am I going to do?*

23

IT TAKES FAITH

Lost in thought, Melanie made her way downstairs. She almost ran into her mom standing in the kitchen. It took her a moment to realize that her mom was not alone. She had her arms around Sybil's mom, who was bawling her eyes out. Totally not something her mom would do with anyone.

"Mom, what's wrong?"

Her mom gave Ms. Arnaud an awkward pat before facing Mel. "I hate to tell you this, Mel. But it's Sybil. She's missing."

Luckily, a chair was by her side when Melanie's knees gave out. "What? No! How do you know?"

Ms. Arnaud wiped her eyes with her sleeve and stared sadly at Melanie. "She didn't come home for lunch today," she said. "Her dad didn't worry until a couple hours passed. That was when he went looking for her. No one's seen her. Plus, her cell phone was lying in the street by the intersection. Her bag was a few feet away in the bushes." Fresh tears began to spill. "We've called the police."

Oh no! thought Melanie, *they couldn't get me, so they've taken Sybil.* Then she remembered the earlier text message. Sybil had tried to contact her.

The three of them stood in the kitchen, too shocked to speak. Melanie felt so guilty.

Just then, her phone rang. It felt as though just thinking about her cell phone had made it ring. She hoped it was Sybil again. But when she glanced down at the number, she did not recognize it. It was a text message. Her mother gave her a stern look. As Melanie put the phone down, she accidentally hit the message button with her thumb. There, on the screen, in big bold letters, was a horrible message.

WE HAVE HER. GIVE US THE RUBY IF YOU WANT HER BACK!

Melanie dropped the phone.

"Melanie!" Her mom shushed her, angry at the rudeness.

"Mom. Oh no, Mom. It's all my fault. Look at the phone."

Melanie sat in numb shock as her mom bent over and picked up the phone.

"Oh dear." Her mom plunked down on a kitchen chair.

"What is it? What does it say?" asked Sybil's mom.

"Melanie, go get Uncle William. These men don't know what they're up against." As Melanie left the room, she saw her mom pass the phone to Ms. Arnaud.

In just a few minutes, Melanie was back in the kitchen with her uncle. They all sat around the kitchen table, urgently discussing the situation. Melanie knew that she needed to spill her guts. She just hoped they didn't think she was crazy—like Aunt Flo.

"Mom? Uncle William? I need to tell you something."

All eyes turned her way. Suddenly her tongue felt swollen and limp.

"I should have told you earlier, but I didn't think you'd believe me."

"What is it, Melanie? Do you know what's happened to Sybil?"

Brave. Be brave, Melanie thought. "It's the ruby. They couldn't get it from me, so they've taken Sybil."

"We can see that from the text," said Uncle William. "The question is why?"

"Well, that's why I didn't think you'd believe me. The ruby, it's...it's magical."

Melanie's mom stood up so fast that her chair toppled backward. "That's enough, Melanie. What do you think this is? Some kind of game?"

Melanie shrank back into her chair. Her voice squeaked. "I'm not lying. It's true."

"Let's hear her out," said Uncle William. "She obviously believes what she's saying."

"Thank you," said Melanie. She took in all their faces. Ms. Arnaud was pasty white, her eyes pink. Her own mom, still flushed, looked like the devil. But Uncle William, he gazed at her with love and concern. She had seen that look before, back when Aunt Flo was alive.

"Here, I'll prove it." Melanie leaned forward so that the necklace dangled from her neck. "Try to take it off."

"Melanie, what nonsense," said her mom.

Uncle William, however, leaned forward and gave the chain a casual lift. His eyes widened, and his grasp strengthened as he realized that he couldn't raise the necklace above her head. "Well, I'll be. She's right. It won't budge."

Dorine White

"Please listen to my story. That's all I ask," said Melanie. By now, her mom had righted the chair and sat nimbly on its edge.

Melanie told them what she knew, all about the ruby, Cleopatra, and hearing voices. "You see, Aunt Flo wasn't crazy. Well, not all that much, anyway."

"Are you telling me you can hear my thoughts?" her mom demanded.

"I can if I try. It's unpleasant listening to people's thoughts, so I try to block it out. Sybil's aunt, Cecile, has been helping me."

Ms. Arnaud's lips thinned.

"Fine. Then what am I thinking about?" asked her mom.

Dropping her mental shield, Melanie focused on her mom. She certainly did not want to read her mom's thoughts. However, when she did, she couldn't help but laugh. Her mom was thinking extremely hard about pink elephants jumping over white picket fences. She closed her shield and grinned.

"Mom, what in the world do pink elephants and white fences have to do with anything?"

Her mom gasped, slapping one hand over her mouth.

"My poor Flo," said Uncle William. "All those years."

"It's OK, Uncle William. Aunt Flo already heard voices before she got the necklace. The necklace just added real voices into the mix. She's OK now anyway."

"What do you mean?" he asked.

"I can see her. I mean, Aunt Flo. She's been watching out for me."

Tears ran down Uncle William's cheeks. "Is she here now?"

"Hold on, let me see." Melanie stood up and looked around the room. She did not see anyone. "Aunt Flo, you around?" she called out.

Turning in a circle, Melanie waited and watched. Then she caught sight of mist gathering behind Uncle William. Suddenly Aunt Flo stood there, a hand on her husband's shoulder.

"She's here, Uncle William. She's right behind you. She's touching you."

William glanced around with teary eyes. "I can't see her."

"I'm sorry. It's probably just with the ruby."

"Tell him it's fine," said Aunt Flo. "It takes too much energy to appear to everyone. My time is almost done, and I don't have much energy left. Ask him to close his eyes."

"She says it takes too much energy to appear, but she wants you to close your eyes."

The ghost hovered in front of William. As he closed his eyes, she gently leaned toward him and kissed his lips. Uncle William's eyes opened with a start, and his hand flew to his lips. "I felt her. She kissed me."

Melanie hopped up and down on her toes. "Yep, that was her."

"Tell him I love him," said Aunt Flo.

"She wants me to tell you she loves you," said Melanie.

Uncle William leaned back in his chair, and his eyes filled with wonder. Her mom sat quietly in her chair, but Melanie heard her thoughts. *What will the neighbors think?* Melanie shook her head at her mom's pride.

"Where's my baby?" Ms. Arnaud demanded.

Time for the rest of the story, thought Melanie. She spoke about the cult and how a girl from Ohio had contacted her.

She told them about the tattoos and the danger they were all in.

"When Jason failed to get the necklace, they must have come up with another plan," said Melanie.

Ms. Arnaud slammed her hand down on the table. "Nobody is messing with my girl. Let's go get them!"

Melanie only wished she could go. "Ms. Arnaud, I only know why they've taken her, not where."

Sybil's mom growled low in her throat.

"I do have an idea, though," said Melanie.

"Well, let's hear it then," said Uncle William.

Facing Aunt Flo, Melanie asked, "Aunt Flo, you know how you came to visit me at the Cerisees' home? Can you do that again? Can you go anywhere you want?"

"Almost anywhere. I'm bound to places near where I lived in life." Then Aunt Flo shook her head. "Yes, I see. You want me to find Sybil. Hmm...New Orleans is huge. Is there anything you can tell me that might help?"

Melanie closed her eyes and pictured Sybil. "She might be wearing my bracelet. The one with the heart locket. I gave it to her as an Easter gift."

"Melanie! You gave her your grandmother's gold brace-let?" Her mother's voice sounded like a high-speed train braking on the tracks.

Melanie looked her mom square in the eyes. "Yes, I did."

Her mother's lips thinned, but she stayed quiet. Melanie turned back to Aunt Flo.

"Your connection to the bracelet should help me find her. I'll do my best." Aunt Flo disappeared.

"What did she say?" asked Melanie's mom.

"She understands. She's going to find Sybil and then come back and tell us where they are."

They all sat back to wait. Mr. Arnaud arrived in a few minutes. He went straight to Ms. Arnaud and held her. They quickly filled him in on the ruby necklace and Aunt Flo. He took in everything with a determined grunt and didn't say a word.

When the cops arrived, the detective made everyone sit in the living room. Melanie was glad Big Feet Cop and Fat Cop weren't there. Melanie sat sandwiched between her mom and uncle. The cop, Detective Larson, appeared annoyed. He tapped his foot with an irregular rhythm as Uncle William told him the story of the ruby.

"You're trying to tell me that this little girl can read people's thoughts?"

"Look, we know it sounds strange, but you've got to believe us," said Uncle William. "Finding Sybil depends on it."

Melanie wondered what exactly to tell the detective. If he didn't understand the mind reading, then there was no way he would believe that she talked to ghosts. Waiting for Aunt Flo was driving her nuts. She had already bitten each of her fingernails down to the pink part.

"All the evidence we have points to abduction," said the cop. "That's the only reason I'm standing here. Right now, we have remarkably little to go on. The Crime Scene Investigation team is working on the kidnapping site. Besides that, all we've got is the text message."

"It's the necklace. They want my ruby," said Melanie.

"That's clear from the message. What we need now is a contact call. We need them to give us the terms and the location for the trade," said Larson.

"That's all well and good," said Melanie, "but they can't have the necklace anyway." She lifted the pendant in a vain attempt at removal.

"What?" asked the cop. "You're unwilling to give up the necklace for the life of your best friend?"

"It's more complicated than that," mumbled Melanie.

"Look, we'll do whatever it takes to get Sybil," said Uncle William, "but your best bet of finding her is right here." He pointed at Melanie. "You need to start listening or we might miss our chance."

"Look, mister," Detective Larson said, throwing down his notebook, marching straight up to Uncle William and standing only two inches from his face, "you need to start listening to me, and no more of this hokey-pokey."

She broke her own rule. Melanie just could not take it anymore. She dove into the detective's thoughts. They were a huge jumble. She could tell he worried about Sybil and wanted to find her. He felt bewildered that Sybil's parents and friends were trying to stall him. Then, Melanie caught a determined, fearful exclamation. *This will not end up like the last one!*

"What happened to the last one?" asked Melanie.

"What?" The detective took a jerky step back from her uncle. He turned toward Melanie. His skin turned ghostly white. "What did you just say?"

Melanie stood up. Enough was enough. She needed to get the cop on their side if things were going to work out. The adults were doing a lousy job of communicating. "It's what you were just thinking." She looked Larson right in the eyes. "I read minds, remember?"

The cop opened his mouth several times, but nothing came out. "Is this a trick or something?"

"No, it's what we've been trying to tell you. Luckily, it's easy to prove. Think about whatever you want, and I'll tell you what you're thinking," said Melanie.

"Look, kid—," started the cop.

"Just do it already," interrupted Melanie.

Detective Larson crossed his arms and frowned, but Melanie caught the thought he was trying to keep hidden.

"It was a little boy last time. His name was Michael. You didn't find him in time. I'm so sorry." Melanie jumped out of his mind before she saw too many details.

The cop stared at her for a solid minute, unblinking. "Fine. For the purpose of this conversation, let's say I believe you. Now what?"

"Well, first—" Melanie broke off as a hazy image began to materialize in the corner of the room. She recognized Aunt Flo immediately. She gestured at Uncle William. "One sec, sir, I need to talk to someone."

She walked over to the corner of the room and stood there, her head tilted to the side as she listened. The cop watched her for a second, and then shrugged, turning toward Uncle William.

"Melanie," said Aunt Flo. "I found her."

"Where?" asked Melanie.

"Well, that's the problem. It's somewhere I never went during life, so I can't tell you exactly. I can only get you close, and then it'll be up to you."

"OK. That's better than nothing. What can you tell me?"

"She's out Route 96 along the marshes. It's way past the last housing development, way into the dark."

"Oh no!" said Melanie. "The only reason people go to the marshes is for gator hunting or getting lost. Thank you, Aunt Florence."

"I'm sorry I couldn't be of more help."

Lost in thought, Melanie returned to her family. Her uncle and the cop were talking about the value of the ruby necklace. She cleared her throat loudly. All eyes turned.

"Do you know where Sybil is?" asked Ms. Arnaud.

"How could she possibly know that? She's been standing in the corner of the room," said the cop.

Melanie ignored him. Instead, she walked over to the cook and gave her a gigantic hug. "I don't know exactly, but I know where to look."

"What?" said the cop.

Melanie raised her eyebrow.

"Right," he said. "Forget I asked. So, where is Sybil?"

"She's out Route 96, somewhere in the marshes."

"You're sure about this?" Larson asked. "I'm putting a lot of faith in you."

"I'm sure," said Melanie.

"Good. I'll call this in, and we'll run a patrol out to look."

"Um," hedged Melanie, "I need to go with you."

Her mom frowned. "Melanie, it's too dangerous. You are not going anywhere near those people."

Detective Larson just shook his head. "This is serious police business. It's not a place for little girls."

"First off, I'm not a little girl. And second, you'll need me. The marshes run for miles and miles. You'll need me to listen for her."

"She's right," said Uncle William. "We don't have much time. We need to surprise these guys. Besides, you'll stay in the car, right Mel?"

"Sure. Whatever Detective Larson thinks is best."

"I'm going to regret this," Larson said, hanging his head in defeat.

24

A FIGHT TO THE DEATH

The daylight faded behind purple clouds. Melanie gazed at the sunset and wished it were just a normal evening, but as she peeked at the back of Detective Larson's head, she knew tonight would stay with her for the rest of her life. She glanced out the back window. Two more cop cars followed their lead.

The patrol car turned onto Route 96, and Melanie took in the forest of trees on the horizon. She shivered in her seat. The marshes were not a place she had ever wanted to visit. The idea of being endlessly surrounded by mossy trees and swamps filled with gators, snakes, bugs, and mud held little appeal. She'd studied state history in school and knew that people used to live along the swamps—smugglers, mostly. Today, their wooden homes stood abandoned, left to the hunger of the marshes. Melanie had a feeling she was about to get a real-life history lesson.

"Do you hear anything yet?" asked Larson.

The road they were on was clear on either side. "I think we need to get a little farther in," said Melanie. The only voices she heard were the cops around her.

They entered the swamp as the last rays of sunshine disappeared. The road changed from pavement to gravel, and the tires crunched loudly as they drove. Melanie tried to remove the sound from her thoughts and began her deep breathing. They traveled along slowly. Next to the side of the road were several old shacks. The vacant homes appeared dark and haunted. Down the road they went, deeper into the marshes.

It came upon her suddenly. One minute there was nothing; the next, she heard Sybil screaming in her head. "Stop the car!" yelled Mel.

Larson hit the brakes, and the tires shot a spray of pebbles into the air.

"They're not along this road," said Melanie. She struggled to tune her thoughts to Sybil's. "There must be another path somewhere to the right. Sybil's thoughts are coming from that direction."

Larson slowly allowed the car to roll forward. About twenty yards down, they found a dirt road branching off from the gravel one. "Can you tell how far down they are?"

Melanie reached into Sybil's mind. Her friend was thinking about the kidnapping. Her thoughts were fuzzy, but Melanie got a lucky break. Sybil had definitely noticed the changes in the road when they'd driven in. After the kidnappers had turned off the gravel, the drive had been bouncy and slow. Sybil had a vague idea that several minutes had passed—but not an overlong amount of time.

"It's not far," said Melanie.

"In that case, we'll stop here and go in on foot. There's no way we could conceal the sound of the cars out there." Larson got on the radio and told the other officers the deal. They parked single file. The other cops got out of their cars. Melanie watched as they opened their trunks and removed gear. Each cop put on a bulletproof jacket. Several pulled out shotguns to accompany their service revolvers. To combat the darkness, they turned on flashlights.

"You stay here," Larson told Melanie. "We'll handle everything."

Melanie wasn't sure whether to argue or not. She wanted to be there when Sybil was rescued, but at the same time, the dark swamp seemed downright scary. "OK, but leave me a flashlight. I don't want to sit here in the dark."

The cops moved out, quiet as foxes on the hunt. Melanie monitored their thoughts as they followed the muddy road deeper into the trees. Things seemed to be going well. She jumped into each cop's mind. They were all veterans and ready for a fight.

Melanie sent her thoughts toward Sybil. Her friend felt terrified. Melanie wanted to tell her it would be over soon.

Melanie, I don't know if you can hear me, but I'm in the swamps somewhere. Oh, I hope that ruby can hear me. I'm so scared.

Melanie dropped her flashlight on the floor. "Sybil," she yelled, but then a feeling of despair filled her stomach. Sybil couldn't answer back.

Sybil's thoughts changed. *What's going on? Something's changed...*

Hope had appeared in Sybil's mind, but Melanie felt the opposite. The kidnappers' muddled thoughts flew at her. They knew the cops were out there. Melanie had to do something.

She grabbed the flashlight and jumped out of the car. She ran as fast as her legs could carry her. In her mind, the thoughts of the cops, the cult members, and Sybil all clashed into chaos. Melanie fought off dizziness as she plunged forward. The thoughts got louder as she got closer.

Bang!

Gunfire sounded up ahead, and one of the cultist's thoughts went quiet. Melanie nearly plowed into a tree as Sybil's terror overwhelmed her.

Lights came into view up ahead. Melanie slowed down and took in the scene as it unfolded. She could tell the cops by their flashlights. They had surrounded the front of a shack. Lights blazed from inside the broken-down dwelling. Melanie knew from the kidnappers' thoughts that they were crawling along the floor, pulling Sybil with them. The cops tightened their net, but Melanie knew what they did not: the cult members had an escape route.

Unseen, the swamp reached up to the back of the shack, and the old porch now hung limply in the murky water. Through the minds of the remaining three cultists, she pictured several skimmers tied up to rotting, wooden posts. They were escaping by swamp!

Melanie worked her way down toward the shack. Carefully she kept herself hidden—she did not want to be shot accidentally.

Bang!

It took Melanie a full thirty seconds to realize that she hadn't been shot. Instead, another of the kidnappers' minds had dimmed.

Then the roar of a large fan sounded in the night air. Ahead of her, the cops surged in front of the shanty, their guns held high. She could hear them yelling into the night. It would do them no good. They couldn't reach the back porch by land. They'd have to go through the house, and Melanie could tell from their thoughts that they were unsure about raiding the cabin, afraid to put Sybil's life in danger.

She stepped into the light, hoping the cops would look first and shoot later. At the same time, she felt Sybil's mind leaving the area.

"They're getting away!" yelled Melanie.

Detective Larson turned her way. "I told you to stay in the car!"

"They're not in the house. They've left." She began running toward the shack. If Sybil got too far away, she would lose her.

"Stop!" yelled a cop.

Melanie ran on, heedless of the danger. A flurry of footsteps followed her. She ran straight through the kitchen, dodging a fallen cultist, and onto the back porch. She stopped fast, avoiding a plunge into the water. The last skimmer floated in front of her. The kidnappers had untied it, allowing it to drift, in order to avoid pursuit. She looked around desperately for a pole.

A loud crack sounded as Detective Larson broke off a piece of the rotten porch railing. Using the wood, he reached out and hooked the watercraft. The large swamp skimmer came to rest beside the house. It rose high into the air, its back fan standing nearly three feet tall.

"Hurry." Melanie jumped onto the boat and beckoned to Larson.

Another cop grabbed the side of the craft. "Where do you think you're going?" he asked Melanie.

"We don't have time for this," yelled Melanie. She glared at Larson. "Tell them, Detective Larson. We have to hurry. They're almost too far away."

Larson stepped onto the skimmer. "The girl goes with me. There's room for one more. Charlie, get on here." A cop in the back stepped forward, rifle in hand.

The air whipped past her face as they sped off into the swamp. All three pointed their flashlights ahead, looking for clues.

Melanie turned toward Larson. "They're much further up ahead. Just keep going until I tell you to stop."

Larson nodded. Charlie shot a look of disbelief at his superior, but he followed orders and sped up. They continued into the deep, dark swamp. Their lights illuminated the water in front of them, but several feet to either side, the reeds grew so thickly that they blocked their view. Melanie knew that the kidnappers could hide anywhere, and they would never be found unless she heard their thoughts. She started to sweat under the burden of responsibility. The cops couldn't help. It was all her show.

Now, far away from the old shack, Mel was only aware of the skimmers running through the swamp in the dark of the night. Suddenly she caught a stray thought.

"Slow down," she called.

Charlie obediently turned down the fan.

"They're hiding in the reeds somewhere up ahead. Go slow. I'll try to point them out."

The boat drifted forward.

"There! There to the right!" Melanie pointed.

A shot rang out. A ping hit the metal rim of the boat inches from her body. She threw herself down.

Peering over the side of the skimmer, she spotted Sybil through a thin patch of reeds. Flashlights glared in both directions. Jason held her tightly. He had a gun to her head—a tattoo on his forearm was dimly illuminated in the moonlight. Melanie didn't need to look closely to know it was the cult's pyramid.

Another cultist aimed a shotgun at the police. He called out into the night, "Let us go or we'll shoot her!"

"Hold on. Let's talk about this," said Detective Larson.

A thought entered Mel's head. Larson was going to shoot the man with the shotgun. She trembled in fear, waiting for the worst. Then, she had a brilliant idea.

"I have the ruby pendant," she yelled.

The cultist swung her way. Larson took the shot. The man's dead body hit the water with a smack.

"I'll trade the necklace for Sybil," shouted Melanie. She stood up shakily in the boat. Jason's eyes held hers. Trembling, she began lifting her necklace off. Somehow, she wasn't surprised when it came off easily. She dangled it in the beam of her flashlight.

"Toss it over here, and I'll let the girl go," said Jason.

Melanie read his thoughts. He had no intention of letting Sybil go free. He'd get the ruby, and then use Sybil to escape. *What should I do?*

Melanie? said a voice in her head. She recognized Detective Larson. *Melanie, I hope you can hear me. I want you to throw the necklace just out of reach of the other skimmer. When you do, drop down. I'm going to shoot.*

"OK!" she yelled in answer to both men. Taking a deep breath, she tossed her precious jewel into the air. She watched it soar over the water, heading for the front of the other skimmer. As she dropped to the floor, she saw Jason lean forward to grab the necklace. A shot rang out, and Sybil screamed.

SPLASH!

Melanie peeked over the rim again. Sybil and Jason were both in the water, struggling to grab the ruby. Blood slowly pooled out around them. She hoped it was Jason's. Melanie's flashlight caught a strange gleam in the water. Two green lights were heading slowly up the swamp toward her friend. Level with the water, the green lights moved with purpose. Melanie let out a shriek.

"Sybil, forget the necklace! Swim for the boat," she yelled.

Detective Larson spotted the approaching alligator. "Swim, Sybil. Swim!"

Sybil wasn't listening. Melanie could hear the determination in her mind. Now that Jason was wounded, Sybil was keeping the ruby, no matter what.

Melanie did the only thing she could think of. She threw her flashlight at Jason's head. It crashed into his skull with a whack. A dazed look rolled over his eyes. It was just enough of a break for Sybil to grab the necklace and swim toward their skimmer. She'd only made it a couple strokes when Jason yelled out. Melanie watched as the two green eyes disappeared under the water behind him. Then, Jason screamed louder, and was pulled under the water in a death spiral. Sybil made it to Melanie's skimmer, barely aware of how close she had come to death.

The two girls huddled together in the bottom of the skimmer. Sybil put the ruby pendant around Melanie's neck, where it settled into place as if it had never left. Both girls were quiet as Charlie steered the skimmer back toward the old cabin.

25

THE NEXT GEMSTONE

When Melanie and Sybil returned to the Dufour house, Melanie noticed Pierre's car outside. When they entered the living room, Sybil flew into her parents' arms. Melanie stood back, happy. She was surprised when two sets of arms surrounded her as well. She looked at Charity and Grace in wonder.

"We would have missed you if something had happened," whispered Grace. Melanie saw Pierre and her mother nod at each other. The night had turned out well, so she decided to hug the twins back, and they all broke into giggles. Melanie knew a friendship was growing, but maybe it wouldn't be so bad after all.

Later that night, Melanie sat in front of her computer. She was talking to Sara via Skype, filling her in on all the gory details. So far, it had been a very sobering conversation.

"Your friend was lucky."

"I know," said Melanie. "I'm just glad she's OK."

"These cultists mean business. We need to find a way to stop them."

"But how?"

"I don't know. If we work together, I bet we can do it."

"Well, we have to try," said Melanie. "So what's our next move?"

"I think we need to find the other stones. Have you had any luck using the ruby?"

"No, but I was thinking about that just before I called. I tried to feel for them, but all I got was a sense of imprisonment. It wasn't pleasant, especially after everything that happened today."

"Just keep trying, and let me know when you get something. I'm going to talk to Claire at the antiques store and see if she's dug up any more information."

"What about your friend, Kainu? What's he working on?"

"Right now, he's back with his dad in Nigeria, helping him recover from a coma. As soon as I hear from him, I'll bring him up to date."

"OK. I'll keep trying to use the ruby, but I've gotta go. It's been a long day."

They said their good-byes, and then Melanie got ready for bed.

"You did well, Melanie."

She peeked up from her pillow. "Thanks, Aunt Flo."

The ghost floated around Melanie's bedroom. "Sweetheart, I think it's time for me to move on."

Melanie sat up against her headboard. "But it's not over. I'm still so afraid...You can't leave now. I talked to Sara Bogus when I got home. We need to find the other two gemstones."

"I wish I could help, but it's not my path. I can give you one piece of advice, though."

Melanie leaned forward eagerly.

"Another ghost with a tattoo joined the group up here, but they've all moved on to another realm. I've been watching them, and before they left, I heard them mention France. I think that might be where the next piece lies. Try the ruby again, Melanie. When you are ready, it should be able to connect to the other gemstones over long distances."

"Aunt Flo, I love you so much. I'm going to miss you."

"My dear, I will always be watching you, and I will love you forever."

Tears sprang up in Melanie's eyes. "Good-bye, Aunt Flo."

"Good-bye, Melanie."

Melanie felt a burst of air, and then all was silent. She wiped the tears from her eyes.

"France?" wondered Melanie with a sniff. She lay back against her pillow, holding the ruby pendant tightly in her fingers. She thought about France, and suddenly she knew. It was a feeling unlike any she'd ever felt, but the images she saw were vivid and clear.

She saw a girl with brown hair and blue eyes and wearing an expensive, silk dress looking into an elegant, sterling hand mirror. The mirror seemed to pulse with radiant energy. It was beautiful, but Melanie couldn't understand why she was so powerfully drawn to it—until she saw the large diamond nestled near the top of the handle. She could hear the girl's thoughts. *Oh, please, s'il vous plaît, let the diamond looking glass work for me. S'il vous plaît...*

Wow! A diamond-studded mirror. I wonder what it does? Melanie lay on her bed and marveled. Now she knew that

the next gemstone was a diamond, and that it was somewhere in France. She knew that the cult was already likely
on its trail and that she was supposed to help. But how?

Sleep didn't come easily, but when it did, Melanie had
peaceful thoughts of Aunt Flo flittering around in heaven.
The warm fuzzies stayed with her the next day. She didn't
know what would happen next, but she was excited to find
out. The hunt for the diamond was just beginning.

Acknowledgments

Thank you to everyone who came out to support me and *The Emerald Ring*.

To my husband Trevor, I love you!

To my children, Emma, Alan, Megan, Camille, Tyler, and Matthew, you are my dreams come true.

Hugs to my sisters, Jeannine and Maureen.

To Angela Morrison and ANWA, you made me believe I could do this.

To my editing buddies, Lauri and Esther, I couldn't have done it without you.

A big thanks to the SCBWI, PNWA, and LDS Storymakers.

ABOUT THE AUTHOR

Dorine White graduated from Brigham Young University, Utah, with a BA in humanities and art history. She began writing at a young age, producing books for her family. Today she spends her time writing children's books, mostly fantasy. Currently, she lives in the beautiful yet rainy Northwest with her husband, Trevor, and six children. You can find her online at www.dorinewhite.com.